STEEL-JACKET

MERLE CONSTINER

SAGEBRUSH
Large Print Westerns

First published in Great Britain by Severn House
First published in the United States by Ace Books

First Isis Edition
published 2019
by arrangement with
Golden West Literary Agency

A catalogue record for this book is available
from the British Library.

ISBN 978–1–78541–678–1 (pb)

Published by
F. A. Thorpe (Publishing)
Anstey, Leicestershire

Set by Words & Graphics Ltd.
Anstey, Leicestershire
Printed and bound in Great Britain by
T. J. International Ltd., Padstow, Cornwall

This book is printed on acid-free paper

CHAPTER
ONE

In the prairie twilight Joe Fugate saw the smudge on the horizon, figured it to be Tuckers Knob, realized he was getting well into the Choctaw Nation and decided to camp for the night. The sprawling Ouachita Mountains would be coming up before long and he wanted to skirt their fringes. Fugate, as near as he could calculate, was about nineteen years old. He had been born back in the bloody days and raised a foundling until he was fourteen in the notorious whiskey store settlement of Earlsboro, hangout of horse thieves and nameless transient gunmen, on the Seminole boundary. He was scrawny, a little loose jawed from a long ago fight with a man with a fistful of mule shoe and sat slumped in his cheap saddle, travel dusty, ragged and sweat blotched. He knew the Oklahoma-Indian Territory country inside out, from the Little Tribes area up in the northeast corner, to the Ouachitas, to Greer County, to the Panhandle. He had just come from Arkansas, no work of any kind, and was on his way to Stinson County, over by Greer in southwest Oklahoma, where, he'd heard, there was a job almost anywhere for a passable cowhand.

His mare's forefeet were in a scattering of smooth pumpkin-sized boulders stretching in a fan up a slope and into the notch of a ravine. Down through the rocks, zigzag, helter-skelter, ran a skein of water hardly wider that his bowie knife. It was a spring-fed stream, he knew, starting from somewhere up in the ravine. It was perfect for a night camp. He moved his mount and pack horse up into the ravine.

He'd gone scarcely a hundred feet when he came to its bowl-like source, and the girl bending over it, on her knees, filling a coffeepot. Alone.

He could hardly believe his eyes.

He looked first to see if she had a firearm, she didn't (women went into conniptions quickly if they were startled) then asked politely, "Any way I can help?"

She jumped a mile. He was mighty glad she wasn't holding a hair-trigger .45.

She was golden haired, frail, very beautiful. She looked to be about seventeen.

"Who are you?" she asked.

"Joe Fugate," he said. "And who are you?"

"Amy Dennis," she said. "And what do you mean, sneaking up on me that way?"

"How can you sneak up on anybody, you mounted, leading a pack horse and over gravel?" he said. "You're the one that did the sneaking. Hiding back here as quiet as a mouse, pretending to fill a coffee-pot, waiting to ambush and rob, likely."

"Talk sensible!" she said furiously.

He thumbed back his old flat-crowned hat, so that it hung by its chin strap at the nape of his neck, and swabbed his forehead with a filthy bandanna. "Your camp nigh here?" he asked.

"Just over yonder," she said and pointed.

"How many in your party?"

"Just me and my pa," she said.

"This is lonesome country for a girl."

She said, "My pa can take care of us."

He felt sorry for her. *My pa can take care of us.* Such ignorance.

He looked at her and liked her and sensed she liked him, too. It made him uneasy and messed him up.

To force a little polite conversation, he asked, "Where y'all from?"

"East Kansas," she said. "We raised pigs."

"Pigs?" he said. He tried to keep the revulsion from his voice.

"They're a gold mine if you know how to do it," she said. "Pa knew how to do it. But a restlessness come over him, and he decided to get into another line of animals. Like cows."

"A very wise choice," said Fugate. "Where you headed?"

"To a ranch called the *Flying 8*, over in west Oklahoma, in Stinson County."

"That's where I'm headed for, too," said Fugate. "Stinson County." Instantly he could have bitten off his tongue.

She was looking at him in a different sort of way. Not hard exactly but carefully. As though she were buying a piece of yard goods.

"You're riding along with us," she announced. "To guide us and so on."

"Oh no I'm not," he said. "Oh, no. Whooie, no!"

She didn't seem even to hear him. She said, "We'll pay you. Of course. Not extravagantly but generously. Though you'll have to wait until we all get to the *Flying 8*."

He turned his mare's head to leave, and said, "Pleasure to have made your acquaintance."

Then he realized that she was quietly desperate.

He asked, "What's wrong?"

"We got lost twice," she said. "And Indians have been following us."

"I believe the lost," he said. "But I don't believe the Indians. What makes you think so?"

"One morning pa and I were away from the wagon hunting and they turned things upside down and stole a ham and two flitches of bacon."

"Pig from the pig farmer," he said.

"It's not funny," she said. "We were short on supplies anyway. That's why we were out hunting."

"Can you hunt?" he asked.

"Can you?" she said.

"Miss Dennis," he said. "I'll come along with you. If you don't try to boss me around."

"I won't. I promise."

"I can't stand bossing," he explained. "My nature suddenly goes unreasonable on me."

They went down a flat gully that forked off to the left and came out into a kind of hollow. It was getting dark quickly now and would soon be moonless night. There

4

was a small wagon with a box-like body built up on its bed, for privacy and against rough weather. The wagon tongue rested on the ground and a team of dappled grays, unhitched from the singletrees and unharnessed, grazed nearby. An old man in overalls was crouched like a spider over a newly laid campfire, puffing it to flame. He scrabbled erect and glared at them balefully as they came up. The fire caught and burst into a scarlet glow from its dead grass and twigs kindling. Bristling, the old man said, "Who is that? Who is that with you, Amy? He been bothering you?"

She said, "No, sir. He ain't been bothering me. And speak nice to him. He's Mr. Fugate. Our traveling companion. He's going along to Stinson County with us."

Fugate said, "Good evening, Mr. Dennis."

"Don't good evening me," said the old man. "You ain't welcome. We don't want no traveling companion. Clear out!"

The girl looked wild with disappointment. She was frightened.

"Please?" said Fugate.

"No," said Dennis.

"I won't get in your way none," said Fugate. "I'll just ride along behind. Sometimes whistling a little maybe, sometimes humming a little maybe. But mainly just riding."

"But eating with us, hey?" said the old man sarcastically. "And grub costs money."

"Pa!" said the girl. "My Redeemer! You never talked this way back home!"

"We ain't back home," said the old man. "As you mighty well know."

"Don't foam up about the food," said Fugate. "I always pack my own supplies. And I'll eat at my own campfire."

"And strangle us some night when we're asleep," said Mr. Dennis. "Who are you? Some young sprout just broke out of the penitentiary?"

He had no idea at all of what kind of country he was in.

Fugate said patiently, "Neither Indian Territory nor Oklahoma Territory has a penitentiary, sir. The nearest penitentiary is across the state line in Kansas. The Territories use that one by agreement. A mighty long trip, you might say."

"I'll say it just once more," snarled the old man. "Don't make me burn no powder. Get on your way!"

Fugate looked around him. "How do I get out of this place?"

"A fine traveling companion you'd have been," said Mr. Dennis. "Can't find your way out of a little hollow."

"I'll show you," said the girl.

Amy and Fugate walked back up the gully.

When they were out of sight of the wagon and the campfire, Fugate said, "I could tail y'all, you know. Stay a little behind and see you and him, but y'all couldn't see me."

"Could you do that?" she asked.

"Hah! I've did it to Kiowas."

"Would you?"

6

"If you'll tell me what it really is that's got you scared. Getting lost and all that is true, I'm sure, but there's something else. More important."

Her eyes bored into him while she made up her mind.

Finally she said, "I'll tell you. We're supposed to own this *Flying 8* ranch, the way I get it. We're on our way there to take over."

"The way you say it," he declared, "I can't make much sense out of it. What do you mean, *supposed* to own?"

"That's the part that troubles me, too."

"Well, let's talk it over a little," said Fugate. "And see can we straighten it out a little. Tell me about it."

"We were back home on our pig farm when pa got this letter. It was from a Mr. Foster Kilburn of Stinson County, Oklahoma, who said he was figuring on selling his ranch out there, the *Flying 8*."

"What post office was the letter from? How was it postmarked?"

"It was postmarked Kilburns. There is a little store and a post office on the *Flying 8*. They do that sometimes in the back country, I hear."

"That's right, they do."

"The property was a mighty nice buy for the right party, said the letter. Post office to bring people into the shop and added to this a fine ranch. He was fixing to retire, said Mr. Kilburn, and he would put the whole works on the block for fifteen thousand dollars gold. Was pa interested? Pa was and wrote him."

"Your pa must be a rich man," said Fugate.

"No," said Amy, "but he's always been a saving man. We lived just outside a village called Hardinville, on the railroad. A letter from Mr. Kilburn said his cousin, a Mr. Brockhaus, was coming through Hardinville on the railroad on his way to Chicago and would stop off. Pa could meet him on a certain date at the Hardinville Hotel, pay over his money and the ranch would be his."

Fugate said, "Sight unseen, from a stranger, in gold! What kind of nonsense am I listening to? What else did the letter say?"

"I didn't see any of the correspondence; Pa just told me about it. Well, the night came for this meeting with Mr. Brockhaus at the village. Pa got the money out of the old horsehide trunk where he'd had it handy and ready and left. He was back at dawn and said we'd bought us a ranch with store and post office."

"Did he show you any papers?"

"No. Pa is always supersecret in his business dealings."

After a moment of utter silence, Fugate said, "I hereby want to state, declare and affirm that I never listened to nothing like this in my whole life."

"Pa was surely excited," she said.

"He must have been, acting that way."

"Now you know why I want you along."

"Can't say as I do. Why?"

"Pa was bilked somehow."

"Was what?"

"Was hornswoggled. He paid out fifteen thousand in gold for something he's never going to get."

Fugate said nothing.

8

"When he finds out," said Amy, "it's going to break his heart, and that's going to break my heart. And there we'll be, friendless, strangers among the alien corn."

"Among the alien cows."

"When the times comes, I've got to have a friend. To hold onto. To give me strength."

"You'll have a friend," said Fugate bleakly. "I'll be right there along with you."

She vanished into the shadows.

He dismounted and went to his pack horse.

He'd long ago, on the trail, learned to make a choice each night, his situation at the moment deciding for him, whether to pitch a quick light camp, a surprise getaway camp or to make a leisurely comfortable camp. Tonight he made a quick getaway camp. Mr. Dennis was a strange one; he might take it into his mind to move on, right this very minute. Listening for wagon wheels starting up on gravel, Fugate unlashed the tarp from his pack horse, to give the beast a little ease, laid it on the ground but didn't unwrap it. He took the bridles and bits from both animals and put them on a short picket. He built no fire but ate the heel of a loaf of bread and a piece of brined beef from his saddlebags. All the time he listened. He heard nothing.

He dozed tensely, tightly, sitting up, his arms around his legs, his forehead resting on his kneecaps.

It was perhaps twenty minutes later when he heard the girl's panicked scream, "Mr. Fugate! Help!"

He came to his feet and was down the gully like a cougar. He thought her father, maybe crazy, had turned on her. He burst from the gully mouth into the hollow and into the midst of a little assembly. He pushed into the group and stopped.

Old Man Dennis was holding three mounted men off with a rifle.

Fugate thought he'd never seen three tougher-looking, more cruel-looking specimens. They were mighty gun wise, too, and careful not to move. One, on a stocky bay, wore a homemade bandolier of frayed canvas. You didn't see many bandoliers in the Territories anymore. Another of the riders, in snagged, old denim pants, wore a shoddy black and yellow striped slub-threaded coat, the ancient cast-off from some bartender probably. The third man, the leader of the group likely, erect and poised in his saddle, had a pouched leathery face and fixed, cloudy eyes. He wore skintight, smooth leather chaps and a gray work shirt.

To Amy, Fugate said, "Who are these men? Why are they here?"

The man in the chaps said, "We're here because the old man brought us in with his gun muzzle."

Fugate said to the girl, "Why did you yell?"

Amy said, "I was afraid Pa would shoot somebody."

"Let's go over this again, slow," said Fugate.

"Pa brought them in," the girl said. "He always goes out a piece from camp and guards up for the night. They came riding up, and he brought them in."

"They were riding mighty sly and wicked," said the old man. "Up to something, sure."

"We seen your firelight," said the man in the chaps. "And was coming in to borrow some molasses for our supper coffee."

"Molasses in coffee!" said Dennis. "I don't believe it. Couldn't nobody do a thing like that to themselves."

"It's a sweetener," said the spokesman. "Raised on it and you get to favor it."

"You know what I think?" said the old man. "I think you just broke out of that penitentiary in Kansas. I think you'uns was bent on robbery and mayhem."

They grinned at him unpleasantly.

"Move on!" said Mr. Dennis. "And watch yourselves in the future!"

"Thank you for the molasses," said the man.

Fugate looked at them carefully. They were a mighty scary trio. And they sure as hell weren't here for molasses.

"Move!" bawled the oldster.

"In this country," said the man, "people don't yell things like *move* to other people. In this country folks comes and goes as they wishes. And does about what the notion strikes them, for that matter. This country don't belong to nobody. It belongs to the Choctaws."

The horsemen walked their mounts away up the trail.

The old man turned to Fugate. "What goes for them goes for you, too. Get!"

Fugate returned to his mare and pack horse.

CHAPTER
TWO

The Dennis family pulled out in the night. Without a creak or axle squeak or the faintest clatter of sliding shale. Old Man Dennis was a fox.

The hollow was empty when Fugate came into it. The campfire ashes were last night's. Dawn was breaking. He picked up the trail.

As the sun came up, and it came up quick and big, the four-inch rims of the wagon wheels left a trail that wasn't too hard to follow.

They must have had a good head start. After a while, from the sign, he realized he was beginning to catch up. He wanted to get close but not too close.

The terrain that he had just passed through had been steep, grooved bluffs and a flat rolling plain. Now he was in a land of gentle hills, streaked here and there with dunes of windblown sand. It was a desolate area, with a few parched oak and ash, and occasionally a bone white sycamore. Mostly though it was prairie and thin soil, sometimes showing bare sandstone, and endless stretches of bluestem grass.

The sun was at midmorning when he came over the crest of an eroded hill and began to hear the rifleshots.

Below him, a short distance out on the plain, was a thimble-shaped stone about the size of a house, with a circle of rock rubble about its base. Near it was the Dennis wagon. Crouched in the rocky rubble was Amy, holding a handgun. Two men sat their mounts a little off, watching her, amused. At their rear, galloping, was a riderless bay horse. Between these men and Amy were two others, her pa, dead on his back in the grass, and a man spread-eagled behind him, with a rifle across Dennis, shooting at the girl as though Old Man Dennis was a dead horse and he was fighting Indians.

Instantly Fugate sensed the situation. The three had attacked the wagon. Mr. Dennis, running forward, had shot one from his saddle, the one from the bay, and had been killed instantly by the others. The man from the bay, wounded, was using the oldster as a shield from the girl's fire. The two mounted men showed no concern whatever over their wounded companion. Horses and men, these were the visitors of the evening before at the Dennis camp.

Fugate freed his pack horse and raced his mare down the slope, shooting.

The two riders left at a dead run.

Fugate came up to the girl and swung to the ground. Flushed, she said, "Mr. Fugate! What brought you?"

"What brought me?" he said. "Ha, that's a good one. Your screaming brought me. I could hear it yonder side of that hill. Mr. Fugate, Mr. Fugate! Help, help! Just like last night."

"It's a lie," she said. "I didn't scream. I didn't call you."

"When we get hysterical," he said kindly "sometimes we don't know what we're doing."

"I never get hysterical," she said.

"That's fine," he said. He had her good and mad now, like he wanted her. She had a bad time coming up. "Stay here. I'm going out to that feller with your pa."

"I'm going, too."

"Then walk behind me," he said. "And walk on eggs."

He drew his gun and went forward across the bluestem.

As they approached, they saw that not only Mr. Dennis was dead; the stranger prone in the grass behind him was dead also. "I'm not surprised," said Amy. "Pa shot him, and Pa's a tolerable good shot. It just took a little time, that's all."

They examined the two bodies. Amy was dazed at the close-up sight of her father but held her self-possession. "Maybe it's just as well," she said. "He didn't have anything but disappointment ahead of him."

"What are you going to do now?" asked Fugate.

"This doesn't change anything," she said quietly. "I'm going on to Stinson County and get what's rightfully ours."

The dead stranger, chunky, brutal looking even in death, with puffy brown lips that hung open showing yellow teeth, was the one with the canvas bandolier. Fugate picked up his rifle. "This gun is a Krag," he said. "It's a fine gun and was the Army gun for a

14

while." He laid the rifle carefully on the ground and took a cartridge from the bandolier. "This is its special shell, and you can't pick up a Krag shell at just any backwoods store. That's why he carried his extra supply along with him in a bandolier."

"Why are you telling me this?" she asked.

"I'm talking to myself," he said. "I'm trying to save our lives. I'm trying to figure it all out."

She stared at him in respect.

He said, "The Krag shell is rimmed. The bullet is 220 grains. It has a soft core with a sheath of harder metal and is soft nosed. It has a walloping muzzle velocity, two thousand feet a second."

"Is that what they call a steel-jacket?"

"That's right."

"So what?" she asked.

"It fires smokeless powder. It would make a mighty fine ambusher's gun."

She didn't say anything but waited.

"My guess," said Fugate slowly, "is that ambushing was this man's trade."

"Does that change anything from our point of view?" she asked wearily.

"It can change things a lot," he said. "If he's a professional and not a common drifter, it can change things a lot."

The others had acted like professionals, too. Unhurried, amused.

Gently he gave her instructions. She went to the wagon, came back with a reddish brown suit, Mr. Dennis's Sunday suit, and handed it to him. She picked up her father's Winchester and went away. Fugate changed the old man's clothes, searched the stranger, finding nothing of consequence. He then went to the wagon himself and got a mattock and a spade; it would be shameful to ask the girl to have brought them. It took him three hours to dig the graves. When he had put in the bodies and filled the holes, the graves looked exactly alike. All graves look alike, he thought bitterly.

It was about one o'clock when he got back to the wagon, carrying mattock, spade and Mr. Dennis's clothes. Amy had a frugal noon dinner cooking. He wasn't hungry, but he cleaned his plate so she would eat.

There were flies on his chipped enamel plate and on his bone-handled iron fork. He knew he was eating from Mr. Dennis's equipment and this didn't make it easier. The sun was fiercely hot. The food was like a log chain in his stomach. He couldn't get his mind off those two graves; Mr. Dennis in his rust brown Sunday suit; the stranger buried with his Krag and bandolier.

When they had finished with the meal and the girl had washed and carefully put away the things, Fugate said, "Why don't you turn around right now and go back to Kansas? I'll ride along and see you there."

"I already told you what I was going to do," she said. "We own that ranch. I'm going to show up and move in."

"I'd like to watch that," he said. And then he asked, "Don't you have any proof, any proof at all, that it was transferred to your father, that he bought it?"

"Pa was very sharp," she said. "There must be proof, good solid proof. Of some kind. Somewhere."

"Let's find it," he said. "Let's search the wagon. Now."

They searched the wagon. Twice. They searched the bedding; they searched all of her father's clothes. They searched her clothes, too, for she said Pa had been a sly one. They looked in the toolbox. They looked under the wagon, up-against the bottom of its bed. In any wagon there is only so much to search. There was nothing.

When everything had been replaced in a neat orderly manner, he said, "Zero. And you don't seem too bothered."

"Why should I be?" she said. "We got right on our side. And the Truth shall prevail."

"Before you left the pig farm," he asked, "what's the farthest you ever traveled?"

"I knew the village like our barn lot," she said. "But most of my traveling, frankly, was from the stove to the sink to the well."

"Let's get away from this place," he said softly. "Let's get started for Stinson County."

She climbed into the wagon seat and picked up the reins. He mounted.

Amy said nervously, "Mr. Fugate, I think I ought to tell you something. I pretty well know the train schedule for the village back home. There wasn't any Chicago-bound train coming through that night, like Pa said."

"There wasn't?"

"No. And that means Pa didn't have any appointment with this Mr. Brockhaus."

He was speechless. He just looked at her.

She said slowly, "Pa could sure lie to me when he wanted. You know what I think?"

"No. But I'd sure be pleased to be informed."

"I don't think there is, or ever was, any Mr. Brockhaus. I think he was just one of Pa's two-faced fibs."

"But why should he do such a thing to you?"

"I'm a female. Time and again I've heard him say 'never tell a female about any important business dealing.'"

"Then what became of the gold?" said Fugate. "You saw him take it out of the trunk and out of the house."

"I think Pa went into the village with it and shipped it to them. Maybe as common freight in a keg of sawdust. That's the tricky kind of way he'd do it."

"Just send it off? Without any guarantee?"

"Maybe a letter ordered him to. He was terrible excited. He was afraid he'd miss a big opportunity. A store and a shop, and a ranch to boot."

"How can my eardrums stand all this?" he asked.

The dappled grays leaned in their harness and the wagon pulled away.

He followed at about forty yards with his pack horse.

He knew if he lived to be a hundred, he'd have nightmares about kegs filled with gold coins and sawdust.

The country changed. The sandstone hills became lower and flatter. The grass, always spotty now, stayed

18

bluestem. You could tell what part of the Territories you were in by just the grass. East bluestem, west buffalo grass. The sides of even the low hills were badly channeled with washes. Fugate's shirt became hot and sticky. Ahead of him, the girl in the wagon drove on and on and paid him no heed. About four o'clock, he saw a fringe of cottonwoods ahead of them; that meant a stream. When they came to it, he yelled and stopped her, and they filled the two water barrels, lashed one on either side of the wagon. They didn't have much to say to each other as they did it. He could see that grief for her father had at last taken her, and he was careful to be casual and matter-of-fact about the operation. He'd kept a sharp eye out and had seen nothing, but he was still uneasy.

All afternoon it had been more gently swelling country, more low sandstone slopes channeled zigzag by washes. The grass was thinner now though, in tufts and hummocks in the sand.

Finally the setting sun was on the western horizon.

He was riding easy in his saddle when the idea hit him.

He went ramrod stiff. It explained everything. The Krag rifle and the ambusher, the violence against the harmless Dennises, everything. Could it be that this Kilburn, now that he had their money, had put killers on them to eliminate them? Swindle them out of their money and erase them before they could complain?

The killing could be actually part of the flimflam.

No complaint, no publicity and he could go on and on.

As a matter of fact, couldn't he have done it before? Maybe many times.

If this was true, one thing was sure. They'd see those killers again.

Every Easterner wanted a ranch these days; it was a kind of epidemic. But how did he bunco them into handing over their money in advance?

What in hell did he say in those letters he sent? Fugate was numbed.

He called, "Hey! Miss Amy! Wait!"

She reined in the dapple grays, and the wheels stopped. He cantered up and spoke to her, his knee by the wagon seat. "Miss Amy, I think we ought to eat and then turn south. Now."

"I was watching for a place to camp," she said.

"I don't think we'd better camp tonight, I think we'd better keep rolling."

"But why south?" she asked. East-west had been her direction, in a straight line — the shortest route to her destination.

"I'll tell you later," he said, deciding not to tell her until he had to.

She caught the sense of emergency. "Just sit your saddle right where you are," she said. "I'll fix us each a sandwich. No need even to light down."

She leaned back over the seat into the wagon and rummaged around into a cedar box, evidently a sort of food locker. She rumaged for some time. Finally, when she handed it to him, it wasn't a sandwich at all. It was a small handful of leftover hominy and a fragment of cheese rind. She didn't get anything for herself.

20

He hated hominy and the cheese was flint hard, but he ate it. He had been brought up to believe it was polite to eat what was given you, and that it was a sin against humanity to ever throw any kind of food away.

Now he walked his mare and pack horse a little to the fore, and they turned south.

Darkness came, and all night he led the wagon by the stars. South.

CHAPTER
THREE

They got a few hours sleep in a scattering of post oaks just before dawn, Amy in the private sanctum of her wagon, Fugate on the ground, ready for action, no blankets. Usually at such a break there would be some kind of breakfast, but she didn't mention it and neither did he.

It was noon, in fact, before she brought up the subject of grub.

She called him back to her and said, "I'm sick and tired of hominy and cheese. Let's try a little of whatever you've got."

"I haven't much," he said. "Not much to be relished by a female."

He got it out, meal and salt pork and dried beans, and they made a regular camp and ate it like a feast. She did the cooking. They were by a stream in a clump of cottonwoods, and the birds were going like a fiddle at a dance.

Afterward, she said, "I'm going to be honest with you. It isn't that I'm tired of hominy. I don't have any anymore. I don't have any food at all anymore. Until this, I haven't actually eaten for a day and a half. We had a little hominy, but I've been piecing it out with a little coffee for Pa."

He was careful not to look at her.

He said, "Nothing to worry about. I'm well stocked." He wasn't; his food was almost exhausted, too.

She said angrily, "Do you think I'm going to live off of you?"

"I hope so," he said.

"Let's go hunting!" she said brightly.

"For snakes?" he asked.

That was the way they traveled, south by southwest, the sun just off their right shoulders during the day, star patterns guiding Fugate at night. Eating meagerly, the girl backing into her wagon every night like a she bear just daring Fugate and the world to tamper with her. The fourth day found them deep in the forests of the Ouachita Mountains.

Finally he explained the situation to her, about the killers, the way he saw it.

She said, "But we've lost them, haven't we?"

He didn't answer. Killers were paid *not* to let you lose them.

The going was terrible at times, not so bad at others. Twice, single-handed, he had to fix a wagon rim. The Ouachitas, he explained to her, took in about all the southeastern corner of the Indian Territory. It was a country of high sandstone ridges running east and west, of valleys with spring-fed streams and forests, forests, forests, oak and long-leaf pine, mainly. Not far to the south was Texas. "If you pass a man on the trail," warned Fugate, "chances are he's a outlaw on the run from the south. Turn your head aside; he won't want to be remembered, and no need to answer him even if he says howdy."

"We have outlaws in Kansas, too," she said primly, reproving him. "I know how to conduct myself."

"A Kansas outlaw compared to a Ouachita outlaw," he said, "is like a house cat compared to a wounded puma."

They traveled just within the cover of the outer mountains, not penetrating the interior fastnesses, moving through ridge gaps and along timbered valleys, following a crude road that Fugate told her had been the old Paris, Texas trail. It was longleaf pine night and day, interminable stands of giant, lance straight trees filtering starlight and sunlight. There was the tangy sweet smell of turpentine, and the forest floor was soft and silent. Occasionally in a shadowed, stony niche by a spring there would be a carpet of pale tan toadstools. It was on the fourth day after Tuckers Knob that they rounded a honeycombed mossy rock, blocking the trail in a tangle of scrub, and came upon the lone horseman. He was just sitting his saddle at rest. His horse blocked their way. He gave them a boyish, friendly grin. Fugate placed his age at about fifteen. He was wearing a gun belt with a bone-handled .44, but was peeling a twig and chewing it and seemed lost in reverie. Amy thought he was charming.

She said, "Howdy." She brought the wagon to a stop.

"Howdy, ma'am," he said. Then asked politely, almost timidly, "Would you people care to take a look at it?"

"At what?" asked Fugate.

"At the roadside yonder," the boy said, and pointed with his thumb.

They looked. A man lay on his stomach with a rifle trained on them.

Fugate knew it was too late; he didn't want to risk Amy; they were caught.

Speaking to Fugate, the horseman said respectfully, "Now please don't cut up. Just do what I say. Take out yore gun, put it in one of yore saddlebags and buckle the bag. I don't know how good you are, but you ain't good enough to try any tricks. Right, Edward?"

The man on the ground called back pleasantly, "Right, Harry."

Fugate put his pistol in a saddlebag and buckled the bag.

The rifleman got up, came forward and stood in the road beside the other. "We're brothers," he said amiably. He was about twenty. "Most people can spot the likeness pronto."

They were red haired and blue eyed, with guileless happy smiles. They were dressed alike in stiff new khaki from some country store, factory creases still showing in their shirt sleeves, cardboard labels of price and size still sewn on their pants' waistbands above their gun belts. They looked to Amy like the kind of boys she used to see back in Kansas at strawberry festivals; they looked to Fugate like something else.

The one called Harry beamed and said, "A young married couple! If there's one thing I admire, it's a young married couple."

"We're not married, I'll have you know," spat Amy.

"Just skylarking, hey?" said Harry. "I admire that even more."

"We're in a bad way for food," said the one named Edward. "We haven't ate since Texas. Sometimes, riding along, Harry has visions."

"We're in a bad way ourselves," said Fugate. "But I was brought up to feed the hungry. We'll share with you. But it'll be a mighty little."

"We ain't interested in no share," said Edward. "We want all you got."

Amy was appalled. She said, "Don't give it to them, Mr. Fugate."

"You got the law on yore heels?" asked Edward. gently.

"No," she said.

"Well, we have," he said. "We'd hate to slaughter young folks about our own age, but we got to get it some way. Fork it over."

Wordlessly, Fugate dismounted, went to his pack horse, undid the tarpaulin and got it for them: a brown paper sack of cornmeal, a couple of pounds of pinto beans, a precious little twist of coffee in a scrap of newspaper and a small hunk of salt pork hardly bigger than a deck of cards. They divided it between them and put it inside their shirts. Edward hopped on Harry's mount, pillion, and they rode away.

After they had gone, Amy said, "Who were they?"

"Texas badmen, like I warned you about," said Fugate mildly. He unbuckled his saddlebag and restored his gun to its holster.

26

"What will we do now?" she asked.

"Rob somebody ourselves."

She looked horrified.

"I was just joking," he said, enjoying her reaction. "Don't worry. We'll get along."

"They didn't know what they were doing," she said.

"Don't you think they didn't," he said.

"Why didn't they take your pistol?" she asked.

Now he was horrified. "They would have, maybe, if they'd had to kill us. But you only filch a gun from a dead man. I think it's in the Bible."

After a minute, he asked, "How much money you got?"

"Two dimes," she said red faced. "How much you got?"

"Four cents," he said. "It's a long way to Stinson County, but they better expect us."

It was later that day they saw the cabin. It was more house than cabin, really, and the first man-made structure of any kind they'd seen for a day and and a half. The trail took a crook and there it was, down in a declivity a short distance ahead of them. Fugate said to Amy, "Stop," and they stopped.

They looked at it cautiously. It was crowded almost flush to the trail side, nestled in the looming trees. It was roofed in shakes — four-foot shingles crudely split from logs — and had a porch with a pole railing. A sign across its front said, SHELLS FOOD BEER. The little store was a relic, probably, still holding on from the days when the trail was in hot use from the land runs. If it had any trade at all now, Fugate decided, it must be mainly outlaw trade. It had a lonesome feel to it.

To their left was an arid creek bed, overhung with foliage. Here, back out of sight, they hid the girl's dapples, the wagon and Fugate's mount and pack horse. He said, "Hand me your father's Winchester." She rumaged around, got it and passed it to him.

He said, "You better come along. I don't like to take you, but I like to leave you worse."

They went down the trail, crossed the porch and entered the building.

Inside, it was cool and pleasantly fragrant from the spice of pines. The shop had once been sizable, apparently, but had been reduced in space by a slab lumber partition at the rear, adding extra room to the living quarters, likely. At their right as they entered was a small plank bar with a shelf and a jug behind it; to their left, against the wall, was a mound of supplies in kegs and crates and boxes and gunnysacks. A fat woman in a starched pink housecoat came from a door at the rear and joined them. She had popping toad eyes, her cheeks were smudged with rouge, and she gave off a fog of perfume. Fugate said politely, "I'd like to speak to your husband."

"I'm chief here," she said. "What can I do for you?"

Fugate handed her the Winchester. She examined it like an expert.

He said, "I want to negotiate it with you."

"It's well-kept?" said the woman.

Fugate nodded.

"I sometimes have parties interested in rifles," said the woman. "What did you expect for it?"

"A little grub," said Fugate.

"Fair enough," said the woman. "Look around."

"She's my wife," said Fugate.

"Howdy," said the woman.

Amy was tongue-tied.

"I'm her husband," said Fugate. "Traveling. Together."

"That's nice," said the woman. "Some don't."

She left the room and came back with two empty sacks.

Amy took them across the room and began filling them. The fat woman watched. Suddenly she asked, "Expecting friends?"

"No," said Fugate. "Why?"

"Through that door, quick," said the fat woman. "We're getting visitors of some kind. I'll handle them."

Amy and Fugate went through the door she indicated and came into a neat kitchen. Fugate slipped out his gun. He shut the door carefully, leaving a narrow crack.

Two men came into the shop; Fugate had seen them before, twice. He'd seen them first at the Dennis's campfire and later in the bluestem when the old man had been killed. One was the man in the striped coat and shabby denim pants; the other was the one in the tight, greasy chaps and gray work shirt. When Fugate caught a slice of their stubbled faces through the door crack, he could see that they were deadly, ruthless. These were the men, all right, and they'd finally caught up with them.

They had probably ridden ferociously, catching sign, losing it, finding it again.

The man in the chaps, the head man of the two, said, "Anybody been through here?"

"What do you mean, anybody?" said the fat woman. "This here's a public highway. They tell me it goes to a place called Paris, Texas."

"I had in mind a girl with a wagon," said the man. "Maybe or maybe not she had a young feller along with her, on a mount and with a pack horse."

"I'm chopping and salting cabbage for sauerkraut," said the fat woman. "That keeps me in the kitchen. How would I know who has went by?"

"You know everything, Mrs. Murchinson," said the man in the chaps. He took out a wad of money from his shirt pocket and peeled off a bank note. "This is twenty dollars, a Double X," he said. "Don't hold back on me."

The woman took the money. She said, "They come through here two nights ago. And bought some shotgun shells. The girl is taking the boy down into Mexico someplace."

"Two nights ago?" said the man. "How could they? Two nights ago they was forty mile north o' here, I think."

"Then one of us is wrong, you or me," said the fat woman. "It boils down to that, don't it?"

"They must really be dustin'," said the man, impressed. "Them wagon wheels must really be spinnin'. We're wasting time, Charlie."

They left. A minute later you could hear their horses on the trail.

When Fugate and Amy came back into the shop, the woman asked, "Did I do all right?"

Amy kissed her, and it looked for an instant there like Mrs. Murchinson was going to cry.

Fugate said, "The wagon is up in that dry creek bed. We'll bring it by, and I'll put in the sacks."

It was while they were on their way back to the store with wagon and horses that Fugate got his inspiration. Mrs. Murchinson was waiting for them on the veranda, the sacks by her ankle.

Fugate said, "This pack horse hinders us. I'm going to leave it here."

"If you mean you're giving it to me," said the fat woman. "I'm not sure I'll take it. I don't expect pay for being human."

Fugate took the tarp bundle from the horse, put the bundle in the back of Amy's wagon and tied the pack horse to the veranda rail. Mrs. Murchinson said to him, "I used to see hard case plainsboys like you in the old days, son. I don't know whether to love you or be terrible scared of you."

"Neither," said Fugate, embarrassed.

"I won't take your horse without at least a one-sided swap," she said. "Will you swap?"

"Depends," said Fugate cautiously, trying to outguess her.

She offered a bushel of sweet potatoes, a burlap sack of onions, a peck of black-eyed peas, a case of canned tomatoes and a case of canned peaches; pursing her lips, she added meat: a smoked pork loin and a side of bacon. He accepted.

The pack horse was worth about forty dollars. The food, perhaps, would come to seventeen dollars. But money wasn't the idea. He would have refused any kind of money.

Amy's face was aglow as he loaded the peaches.

She was already eating them.

Immediately they left the Paris trail and turned west.

That night, over a supper of baked sweet potatoes, fried pork and canned peaches, he explained his plan to her.

They were near the southern edge of the Territories. The boundary was the Red River. There was an old Red River trail from the Ouachitas west toward Stinson County. His plan, he explained, was to use this ancient trail as their general guide. Sometimes they would go on it, sometimes above it, sometimes below it. They could count on their pursuers backtracking on them and taking up their sign again, and this just might befuddle them. This would take them through some pretty primitive country, through some pretty unfriendly country where travelers were often considered prey, pure and simple, but all told it was their most direct route and they'd better chance it. "We have nothing much to really worry about," he said. "We're well stocked with peaches." It would take them south of the Arbuckle Mountains, out of the Indian Territory into Oklahoma, south of the Wichita Mountains and west to Stinson.

"To Stinson County and the *Flying 8*," she said.

"Such are my fondest hopes," he said.

She looked at him quickly. "It could be bad, eh?"

"I'll tell you no lies," he said blandly. "It could be."

"How long do you think it will take?" she asked.

"A week or two, or something," he said vaguely. "Let me spear you another piece of pork?"

She shook her head and handed him a little wad. "What's this?" he asked.

"Twenty dollars," she said. "In one dollar bank notes and silver dollars. The same amount to the penny those men paid Mrs. Murchinson. She'd wrapped it up in cheesecloth so we wouldn't miss it and put it in the sack on top of the potatoes. You'd better carry it."

For a while neither of them said anything. Then Amy said, "Mrs. Murchinson is a wonderful woman, isn't she?"

He said yes she was.

Amy asked, "Was your mother like that — wonderful?"

Expressionlessly, he said, "How would I know?"

"Didn't your mother raise you?"

"My mother went to San Francisco. I was raised by a trash bin in Earlsboro, behind the Happy Hour Saloon."

"I see," she said in a faint voice.

"Don't throw off on it," he said coldly. "There are worse things than trash bins."

CHAPTER
FOUR

"This is the old Red River Trail," said Fugate, about noon next day. "There are names in this neck of the woods like Island Bayou and Frogville and Boggy Creek. The river itself is just a stone's throw to our left."

"Goodness," she said. "This doesn't seem like a good place to raise cattle. I hope Stinson County and my *Flying 8* aren't like this."

Her *Flying 8*. She had already moved in.

"No," he said patiently. "Stinson County isn't like this at all. And they raise enormous cows. Bigger than jackrabbits."

She looked startled. "I should hope so!"

"Take my word for it. They do."

A lot of the time now he rode with her on the wagon seat, driving for her, his mare on a lead at the tailgate.

As they had left the Ouachitas, the land had descended in flat, broken steps, channeled and eroded, but they were really in the bottoms now; and to Fugate, who liked sand and sage maybe sprinkled with a little cactus, it was miserable damp country. The old river trail had once been much used, and the wagon had no trouble on it.

At first, sometimes, they were close enough to the river to see the mud flats and sandbars, but later it was just long stretches of woods: tupelo, gum and cypress. These ancient forests along the trail, like beads on a string, would occasionally break off, and there would be a few miles of sun hot dunes and mesquite and scrub tamarack; and then would come the great cavern of trees once more. The cypress or the gum growing maybe forty feet tall it seemed. There were magnolias, too, and drifted sand and pecan. Where there was undergrowth it was dense and mainly hedgy osage bush.

They were passing through an open space of low mud mounds covered with swamp vines, when Fugate said, "Dead ahead is a sorry little settlement on a sorry little creek. We'll pass it by. There's no use of our seeing any more people or leaving any more track than we have to."

He turned the team of dappled grays abruptly to the left, riverward, into the cypress.

For the next few hours it was trees again, forest and forest floor, half-light, insects and the croaking of frogs. Just before sundown, they came into a little burnout, a little open space, with weeds and charred stumps and a little log cabin. The thick stand of surrounding timber made it like twilight. The wagon was almost up to the cabin before they realized it.

At the far side of the open space, perhaps fifty feet from the cabin, three Indian men and two Indian women sat in the green shadows under the gum trees silently watching them. "Chickasaws," said Fugate.

"We've left the Choctaw country and are in the Chickasaw Nation."

"Are they peaceful?" she asked.

"Of course."

"What are they doing here?"

"I don't know," said Fugate. "It makes me uneasy. I don't think we'd better stop."

A white man came out of the cabin toward them, putting his hands on the wagon harness, stopping the team.

Fugate said, "Are we on the river trail?"

"You're a heap south of it," said the man. "You're lost."

He was about fifty, serpent faced, dressed in droopy green cotton clothes and a little more than half drunk. He hadn't been giving drink to the Indians, though, or they would be drinking, after him for more or asleep. And they sure as hell weren't asleep; you could almost feel their eyes.

"I'm Willie Tesser," said the man. "Did I catch your name?"

"Mr. and Mrs. Ernest Harlowe," said Fugate. "Would you step back a little so I can get by. And that's a bucking horse you got your hand on."

Tesser stood back and asked, "Where you headed?"

"Beaver County," lied Fugate, in a tone that said he didn't much care to hang around and talk. Beaver County, the Panhandle, No Man's Land was the projection of Oklahoma, up in the northwest corner.

"You sure got a long trip ahead of you," said Tesser. "What's your business up there."

36

"If we got a long ways," said Fugate, taking the reins more firmly in his palm, "we better get started."

"How you fixed on money?" asked Tesser.

"You know better than to ask a question like that," said Fugate.

"Travelers," said Tesser, "especially new wed ones, cart along with them a lot of stuff they'll never use. If you have any such, I'll take it off your hands for spot cash money."

"No," said Fugate.

"Spot cash money," said Tesser. He looked avid and mean.

He went to the back of the wagon and began picking things up, looking at them and putting them down.

Fugate got down from the seat and came around to him. "Get your paws out of there," he said softly. Tesser obeyed.

Fugate, speaking quietly so the girl wouldn't hear, said, "I was born in Earlsboro and raised in the Territories, both of them. I'm not a pilgrim."

"Why tell me?" said Tesser.

"Just a warning," said Fugate.

"Warning against what?"

"Don't try to waylay us after we've gone."

Tesser looked a little frightened. "Why should I do that?"

"I relish gunplay as much as you do," said Fugate. "And maybe a little more. I know I've seen more."

"I don't relish gunplay," said Tesser.

Fugate returned to the front of the wagon and swung back into the seat. They drove off.

After they had left the cabin and were again well into the forest, Amy said, "I heard you two talking. What were you saying?"

"I asked him the quickest way to hit the river trail again."

"What was going on back there?" she asked. "The Indians and all?"

"All I can give you is my opinion."

"That's good enough for me."

"I'm mighty sure that cabin is a Indian trading post," he said.

"I've heard of them. We know about them back in Kansas."

"I mean an *illegal* trading post. Legal traders must be licensed by the Commissioner of Indian Affairs and passed by the Bureau. They must have certificates of good character. Riffraff can steal Indians blind. The offense of running an illegal post is severely punishable and should be. Only a skunk would do what they do. But Bureau inspectors, acting for regular agents, are always on the lookout for them. Did you see Mr. Tesser's eyes light up when he first saw us? We meant supplies, untraceable supplies to him."

She didn't say anything.

"His problem is not buyers," said Fugate. "He's got a whole tribe of buyers. His problem is getting stock in a way that won't tip off the inspectors."

"He'd be greedy for everything we have," said Fugate. "And everything we are wearing. Even down to the nice buttons on that dress of yours."

"I'm glad you told him no," said Amy.

"Well, that's what I told him," said Fugate. "No."

Now they turned north again, north by west. They came to the river trail and crossed it.

They ran into some country that seemed almost unpassable — matted briars, tangled brush, a maze of tumbled stones — but they made it. This country was crisscross cut with sharp ravines and thick with wild grape and wild plum. Two days after they'd left the trading post, they were on a sandy plain.

Here they began to really make good time. It was desolate terrain, limestone, sandstone and runty blackjack oak, with a blistering sun, but Fugate liked it. "Soon we should see the Arbuckle Mountains to the north," he said.

He always said "soon" to everything to keep her spirits up.

It was three days later before they saw them.

They saw them midmorning one day in the near distance on the horizon, sticking up from the surrounding plain in lumps of granite and shale, sandstone and limestone. Fugate said, "They're very old, a school teacher once told me. They look tired, don't they? They've been beat down until they're only six or seven hundred feet high."

He'd been watching for water, and late that afternoon they found some.

They came upon it unexpectedly in the notch between two low grassy escarpments branching out in fingers from the mountains. There was a stream and a pool and a cluster of trees. Around the pool were fern fronds and in the pool on a log was a small scarlet-headed turtle. Bird song came from the trees and the shade was cool. They filled the water barrels from the pool, decided to have supper and ate. They were half decided to camp here for the night, when a man came around a clump of osage and said, "Don't move. Man or woman, I'll blow you open."

They turned and stared. At the moment Amy was by the wagon, Fugate by the pool.

The man was heavy with muscle. He had bleary eyes and wore no shirt, just an old vest over his bare chest, and below his ancient cavalry pants his shanks were hairy. He wore Chickasaw moccasins. He held an old .58 caliber percussion cap Springfield rifle, likely loaded as a shotgun, Fugate decided.

The man spat a sliver of tobacco juice.

Fugate said, "Who are you?"

"Fernando O'Toole, a sheepman."

Fugate asked, "What you got against us?"

"To start off with, you're trespassing on my winter grazing."

"In the first place," said Fugate. "This isn't winter."

"I kin tell that, can't I?"

"And in the second place," said Fugate angrily. "This can't be your grazing. It's held by the Chickasaws."

"Them and me have got arrangements."

"You make arrangements like that," said Fugate, "and you'll be looking at a marshal's badge. Bureau of Indian Affairs strictly says no grazing or timber cutting on Indian land."

40

"I'll take care of that," said O'Toole. "I've took care of it before."

Fugate had a suspicion he could. The administration of Indian law was mighty lax at times, not to say openly corrupt.

O'Toole said, "What I want to know is how much in dollars are you and Miss Dennis here worth at a sheriff's office?"

Miss Dennis.

Fugate took a deep breath.

Casually he asked, "How come you know the lady's name?"

"Don't worry about that," said O'Toole.

Harshly Fugate said, "Miss Dennis, we've run into some kind of a mad dog. That gun of his just shoots once. He's got his bead on *me*. If he switches to you, I'll shoot. If he blasts me, let him have it with your derringer, both barrels."

O'Toole looked confused. "I don't see no derringer," he said.

"The world would be better off with a man like him dead anyways," said Fugate.

"I won't need both barrels," said Amy.

"Use 'em anyhow," said Fugate.

O'Toole dropped his Springfield. It fell in the grass across a tussock of pale blue wild flowers.

"Throwing away your weapon won't help," said Fugate in his ugliest voice, his voice of bluff. "I half got it in my mind to kill you anyways." Amy gaped at him.

Fugate said, "Sheepman, I'm going to say it just once more. How come you to know the lady's name?"

"Two riders passed my shack this morning," said O'Toole, now trying to placate, trying to oblige, "and described her and asked me had I saw her?"

"Was one of them wearing tight chaps and the other a striped coat?" asked Fugate.

"That's right, that was them."

They'd picked up the trail at Tesser's trading post probably, Fugate decided, and had overshot them in their hurry. They'd be back. They'd be working their shuttle smaller and smaller and finally catch their prey. Any horseman that can read sign can catch a clumsy wagon.

"Who did you think they were?" asked Fugate.

"Law officers," said O'Toole. "And that there must be a dodger out on the lady. And that there must be money in it."

"And you didn't see no reason why you shouldn't collect that money yourself?"

"That's right," said O'Toole. "Who is she, and who were they?"

"She's the daughter of a pauper pig farmer, deceased," said Fugate.

"Pig farmer?" said O'Toole, wincing. "Gah." He blinked, half bowed, and added, "No offense intended, ma'am."

"They weren't law officers," said Fugate. "The man in the tight chaps is Miss Dennis's disappointed lover. He's chasing her, pressing his suit, as the saying goes."

"Who are you?" asked O'Toole.

Shyly Fugate said, "I'm her real beloved. I'm her chosen."

42

Amy turned purple red in fury but remained silent.

"Shall we put it down to a mistake and let bygones be bygones?" asked O'Toole.

"Suits me," said Fugate.

"Kin I pick up my gun and leave?" asked O'Toole.

"Why not?" said Fugate.

"It was a pleasure meeting you," said O'Toole. He picked up his Springfield and left.

CHAPTER
FIVE

"No more weaving and looping for us," said Fugate when they were alone. "No more trying to take a route that will out-trick them up and down and sideways, like we have been going. From now on we go straight as a die. From now on we make a beeline for Malloy."

"What's Malloy?" she asked.

"The town's that the county seat of Stinson County," he said.

She didn't even know the county seat.

"Is it far from the *Flying 8?*" she asked.

"That's one of the things we'll have to find out," he said. Along with a good many other things, he thought.

She said tensely, "We could ride night and day. You could sleep in the wagon whilst I drove and the opposite."

"I don't think we're down to that yet," he said, trying to soothe her. The fact was, it might damned well be to late for that. Too late for a race.

They harnessed up and drove away straight as an arrow, a little north of due west.

Now that their goal was solely distance, they no longer went out of their way to avoid hinterland settlements and made good time. Not as good as their mounted followers could make but mighty good time for a wagon. The big thing in long-distance wagon driving, Fugate explained to her, was not speed, which brought only breakdowns and trouble, but a careful, steady pace, always with an eye on the condition of your team.

"We still in the Chickasaw Nation?" she asked the next morning.

"Yep," he said. "But almost out of it. Then you can blow your whistles and ring your bells. We'll be in Oklahoma."

"In Stinson County?"

"One county away from Stinson."

"What's the big difference between these two Territories, Indian Territory and Oklahoma Territory?" she asked.

"Law. Government. At least that's the way it seems to me. In the Indian Territory you have the Nations. In Oklahoma Territory, they're already organized, set up, you might say, to come in as a state, with counties and county seats and such."

This was an area of red clay and low hills. Sometimes they crossed short grama grass, sometimes streaks and patches of sand grass. The trees they passed now and then were largely white oak. Occasionally at first, and more and more, they saw sage.

"That's what I like," said Fugate. "When I see that I know I'm getting home. Sage."

It was the kind of sun he liked, too. A sun that curled up leaves and peeled off a tenderfoot's skin. A kind of sun that when your eyes fought the distance, the distance fought you back in a dazzling blind kind of a way.

One morning in the gray light, just after they'd finished breakfast, as Amy was stowing the plates and utensils in the wagon, Fugate said, "Miss Dennis, did you ever see a dog or a pack of dogs 'mill' stock?"

"I can't say as I ever did," she said. "I don't even know what you're talking about."

"A dog gets some cows together, maybe a dozen or so cows, and gets them going in a big circle by nipping their heels. Round and round they go, single file, the dog yapping and nipping, and the cows crazy scared. All this yapping and nipping is done from behind."

"No, I've never seen that. And I don't want to."

"They do it sometimes with mules in a barn lot."

She looked at him and waited for him to make his point.

"That's the way wolves kill in a sheep flock, too," he said. "From behind."

"What are you saying?" she asked.

"I'm saying this," he said. "We're not going to run from those killers anymore. While we're running, we're helpless. We are going to pick a place and turn around and wait for them. We're going to face them down."

She looked stupefied. She said, "Can you handle them?"

"Can't you? You're the Big Hunter. I'll hold the horses."

Fugate looked for the kind of place he wanted as they went along, leaving wagon rim sign in the sand

and soil that a blind man could follow; he sought an ambush place, a hill with a little scrub, maybe. They could put the wagon behind the hill and wait on the hillside. Fugate had an idea they wouldn't have to wait long.

But they passed no hills. The country was rises and swells and endless grama grass. Grass and duned sand and blights of bone smooth red clay.

About three o'clock they started an ascension of slopes, so gentle in their grades that the wagon hardly responded to them, and came out at last on a shelf of arid clay.

Ahead of them, for maybe a hundred yards, the grassland fell away in a slope of railroad tracks. Railroad tracks running north and south, from horizon to horizon. Directly facing them was a group of three wooden shacks, almost at the tracks, almost at the tie ends.

"What are those buildings?" asked Amy.

"Two of them are work sheds, with tools and things for the trackwalkers," he said. "And the other with the stovepipe sticking out through its side is their bunkhouse. All of them will be empty now. They're just used when a crew is working by."

"What railroad is that?" she asked.

"The C, R I and P," he said. "The Chicago, Rock Island and Pacific. We're almost in Oklahoma Territory!"

"We are?"

"For more than a hundred miles, or there abouts, that railroad runs up along the border of the Chickasaw

Nation. Not exactly the border, though, the Nation stretches the other side of it in a five or ten mile strip, varying. Cross the tracks, cross that little stretch of country, and we're in an Oklahoma county."

"Not in Stinson County?"

"No, but not far from Stinson."

"Shall I race the horses?" she gasped. She was driving.

"No, we won't give them that satisfaction," he said. Then he added, "If you're going to race them anywhere, you better race them back to Kansas."

Nevertheless, she snapped the reins and brought the dapples to a brisk trot.

They had nearly reached the shack with the stovepipe, the bunkhouse, when Amy hauled her team to a skidding stop and threw on the brake.

On their way down the slope, one of the toolsheds had been blocking their view of the bunkhouse door. Now that they were almost on the building and their view was unobstructed, they saw the two horses standing sleepily by the bunkhouse door, a liver-spotted gelding and a fine black with a blaze between its ears. They'd seen those horses before, twice. They were the mounts of the killers who had been pursuing them.

The door to the bunkhouse was closed and there was no human in sight. The wagon was at rest dead center on the little circle of sheds, scarcely forty feet from the tired-looking horses.

"I think I'll take your advice," she said. "I think I'll race for Kansas."

"Wait here," he ordered. "Don't leave the wagon."

He got to the ground from the seat.

"What are you going to do?" she asked tensely.

"I'm going in and talk to them," he said gently.

"Why? Please don't."

"Miss Dennis —"

"Call me Amy."

"Miss Amy," he said. "I don't like to be done this-away."

He walked toward the door and passed the horses, rifles in saddle scabbards.

The door had been locked with chain and padlock; now the chain hung limp, and the door was slightly open. He listened for voices from within but heard nothing.

A gunshot crashed from behind him and the door-frame frayed into splinters by his cheek. He whirled.

The killers must have swung around to intercept them and had been pilfering the place, passing the time, while they waited.

The man in the tight greasy chaps was by the wagon. He had reached up to the seat, had sunk viselike fingers into Amy's upper arm and was trying to haul her to the ground. Like a dog would pull a panther from a limb. Amy, her mouth clamped shut, wasn't making a sound, but she was giving him hell with her heels. Her nose was bleeding and so was his.

Between the wagon and the bunkhouse, right on top of Fugate, was the other man, the one in the black and yellow bartender's coat and ragged denim pants. He was running, stumbling, toward Fugate, highly agitated, spastic, firing as he came.

Fugate shot him. As he went down, Fugate shot him again.

Fugate's revolver was a Colt .38–40, and its cylinder was loaded with Winchester rifle cartridges. It didn't miss often, and when it hit, it hit like a train wreck.

The man by the wagon released Amy and stepped back, his hands carefully chest high, away from his gun butt.

"Grab it," said Fugate lazily.

"With your'n out, and you a expert?" said the man. "Not likely."

Fugate said, "Got a rope, Miss Amy?"

"A good strong clothesline," she said. "Will that do?"

"That'll do fine," said Fugate.

"What are we talking about?" asked the man.

"A hanging," said Fugate. "I'm fixing to hang you."

"You mean it?" asked the man. "Or are you just tryin' to goad me into drawin'?"

"I mean it," said Fugate. "You been caught red-handed girl mauling, and that's agin the Law of the Lord."

Looking a little disturbed, the man said, "You a gunfighter and one of *them* lunatics, too?"

"Amen," said Fugate. "Would you like a short order hymn before we start the festivities?"

"You don't mean festivities," said Amy, poker-faced. "You mean Judgment."

"What kind of maniacs are you?" asked the man.

"They's a little dust on the hammer spur of your gun," said Fugate. "Would you care to take the ball of your thumb and brush it off?"

"I sure as hell wouldn't," said the man.

"Would you care to give me your name?" asked Fugate. "Any old name that comes to mind?"

"I'll give you my real name," said the man earnestly. "I know when the water begins to get deep. It's Dave Lawson."

"Hired gun?"

"That's right, Reverend."

"And the other fellow," said Fugate. "The one yonder that crossed my line of fire?"

"A dumb meat head I picked up in a saloon, to my regret."

"How are things at *Flying 8?*" asked Fugate pleasantly.

Lawson said stonily, "What's a flying 8?"

"The *Flying 8* is a ranch," explained Fugate patiently. "I've decided to let you go. For one reason. I want you to go back to Kilburn and tell him we're moving in on him. Why didn't you kill the girl just now when you had the chance?"

"Why should I?"

"That was your job, wasn't it?"

"Then I'd have done it," said Lawson. "Can I go now?"

"Go," said Fugate. "And take your pal's horse with you."

They watched him walk to his blazed black, mount and leave.

Amy washed her face and then they, too, left. In the sky carrion birds were gathering over the cluster of sheds. The wagon bumped over the railroad tracks. An hour or so later, Fugate said, "We're in Oklahoma."

Breathlessly, she said, "At last!"

"That's right," he said. "At last. Right in the middle of the hornet's nest. Smack in Mr. Lawson's country. Smack in Mr. Kilburn's country."

She wasn't listening.

She said, "I don't care what kind."

"What kind of what?" he asked.

"What kind of curtains they have in the bedroom of the *Flying 8*," she said. "I'm going to change them. I brought along my own."

Slowly, the nature of the terrain underwent another change, and the girl mentioned it. Happily, Fugate said, "That's right. This here is real western country."

They were still in interminable, undulating low hills, but the grass was blue gray buffalo grass now. They passed through lots of cattle, and they were fine-looking, well-fatted stock. Sometimes it was grassless, though, with bare, sun-pounded dirt and rocky outcrop and dusty mesquite. There was an occasional dogwood or redbud. Mainly, it was gentle rolling, low, treeless hills. When they filled their water barrels at a stream, they found cottonwoods and elms and willows.

There were little ranches everywhere, and settlements and villages and roads.

52

An old stage pike was going in their direction, so they followed it. They no longer tried to mix up their trail or to keep hidden. "Look at that tumbleweed," said Fugate proudly, as though it were his favorite grandchild.

"I wonder what that man Lawson is doing right now," she mused.

"I hope he's on his way to the *Flying 8* to give Mr. Kilburn my message. But I doubt it."

"What then?"

"He could be in another saloon, trying to pick up another meat head like his partner in the black and yellow coat. To have another try at it, and this time finish the job. When men like him hire out on a job, they got to finish it. Or the word gets round, and they're nothing."

"What job?" she asked. "I don't understand any of this."

No matter what he'd told them back there, his job had to be to kill her.

Fugate, looking baffled, shook his head.

"Your guess is as good as mine," he said.

"Mr. Fugate," she asked. "Were you ever like that man Lawson?"

"I truly hope not," said Fugate.

"I mean were you ever a hired gun?"

"Oh, that?" said Fugate. Lying happily, as though in pleasant memory, he said, "Many and many a time. In my olden days. Oh, them were the joyous times!"

"Consider yourself hired again. By me."

"Hired?"

"For when I take over the *Flying 8*. I might need one of those hired guns."

"You might at that," said Fugate gravely. "But I got to say no."

"Why not?"

"Because I don't want to, that's why not."

"We'll discuss it again," she said serenely. "When you're in a better humor."

CHAPTER
SIX

Next day, a little before noon, Fugate said, "This old wagon has had too many miles. The linchpin on the left rear wheel is about to shear. I looked in the toolbox, but your daddy didn't have a spare."

The linchpin, she knew, was the pin that held the wheel to the axle. She said, "What shall we do?"

"We're coming into a town by the name of Peskar," he said. "We'd best stop and get one there."

"Will they have one?"

"Any blacksmith can make one," he said. "Peskar has about two thousand people."

"Goodness!" she exclaimed.

"It has two railroads and is a kind of cattle link between Texas and the north country."

"I'd like to view it," she said.

He nodded. He saw no need to mention that it was mighty tough.

Before they came into the town proper, they began passing huts and shanties in the mesquite on its outskirts. These gave way to better buildings, dwellings, of sun-warped lumber, painted blue and brown and white, with porches sometimes, and gingerbread eaves and low picket whitewashed fences. Children played;

and you could smell noon dinner cooking: coffee boiling, potatoes frying and pork chops sizzling in hot kitchen skillets. She sighed rhapsodically.

"Like it?" he asked.

"Of course, I like it," she said. "But I prefer my *Flying 8* ranch."

The tracks of both railroad lines came down Main Street, each with its little station and loading platform, one on the north, one on the south. The offices and shops and saloons and dingy hotels along the sidewalk on each side faced the rails. There was about every kind of buggy or wagon or buckboard you could imagine tied at the continuous double hitchracks. Some were spanking fine and some were old and broken down; and the same could be said for their teams. Bales and crates and barrels, in pyramids, and packing cases lined the sidewalks before the show windows. "Whee-oo!" said Amy. "I wish Pa could have seen this. He'd never been any place but Chicago."

They saw three blacksmith shops, came to one they liked: *Chas. Tindle, Work Best, Prices Cheapest,* drove into its barnlike interior and got down from the seat. A lanky sharp-eyed man with a dressed cowhide roped about his middle came forward.

"Traveling a bit, I see," he said. "Them old spokes really show stone cuts. What can I do for you?"

Fugate told him. "Can we leave our wagon here and come back for it later?" he asked. "We want to go to a restaurant and eat."

"Why, shore," said the smith. "Gittin' a mite tired of campfire food?"

"I like campfire food," said Fugate. "But we kind of long for something fancy."

Amy fussed with her clothes.

Fugate said, "What would be the restaurant of your selection for us?"

"The *Bluebird*, next to the *Stockman's Rest Hotel*," said the smith promptly. "Their food is passable, and they won't stick you because you're strangers. I'll keep 'em for you, if you like."

"Keep what?" asked Fugate.

"Yore gun and bowie knife. This is a no-weapon town, and we got a aspirin' young sheriff with more ginger than patience."

Fugate hesitated a long hard moment. He seemed stiffened into rock. Finally he handed them over.

"You can pick 'em up when you come back," said the smith.

Outside, Fugate said to Amy, "Go to the *Bluebird* and wait. I'll be there shortly. I want to buy me some purchases. Unless you want to come along?"

"I don't want to come along," she said. "I'll wait."

At the barbershop, he bought a broken old razor, bone-handled. Sixty-five cents. A block away, he put it in his hat.

He then headed for the nearest of the two depots.

In the depot, he sent a telegram: County Clerk, Malloy, Stinson County, Oklahoma. *Would much appreciate you telegraphing me collect Cottonwood Jc. the following information.* (Cottonwood Junction was a fork in the railroad tracks on the route, about a half day west.) *Am interested in buying from a Mr. Foster*

Kilburn of your county his Flying 8 ranch and the Kilburn Post Office and store thereon situated stop would you consider this a good investment? Signed, John Thomas Brown.

He paid the agent and went into the sunlight.

A man walked up to him and asked, "Passing through?" and Fugate nodded.

He said, "I'm J. J. Connery. Sheriff."

He was about twenty-five years old, scrubbed, starched and wiry. He was hard jawed and hard eyed but not unfriendly. He wore a gun. Fugate had a feeling he was a good man at his job.

He touched Fugate's empty holster and empty bowie sheath, just sort of checking.

Fugate made no comment.

"That's right," said the sheriff. "You won't need weapons here. If something comes up, call me. Hear?"

Fugate just stood there and looked at him.

Silently.

"Welcome to town," said the sheriff.

"Howdy," said Fugate.

The sheriff strolled away.

Amy was sitting at a table in the back of the restaurant when he got there. She was staring at the cheap ware and the thick china. She was nervous at being so public and showed it.

She was overjoyed at seeing him. He sat opposite her.

She said, "Your purchase, your package?"

He patted his pocket. "You'll see," he said.

The waiter appeared and took their order. He said, "How many?" How many, not what would you like. Fugate said, "Two. Both of us." The waiter left.

Amy said, "Aren't you going to take off your hat?"

"Why?" asked Fugate.

"It's the right thing to do," she said. "It's polite, the hat."

"In Kansas, maybe," he said. "Here we take 'em off when we sleep, and only sometimes then. Remember what them old-time folk used to say, 'keep your powder dry and your hat on.'"

"You just made that up," she said angrily.

The waiter came with an enormous tray of food, and put it on the table before them, item by item: succotash, pumpkin pie, coffee, biscuits, butter, strawberry preserves, boiled cabbage, great hunks of steamy chuck roast, mustard, horseradish, fried potatoes with onions, buttered beets, a tureen of raisins and rice. Fugate paid him.

When they were alone again, they ate.

After they'd finished, she leaned back in her chair, gave a dainty little hiccup and said, "I feel like I could rush out and chop a cord of wood."

He looked jolted.

"That's what Pa always used to say," she remarked.

He looked relieved.

As they were leaving, he said, "You go back to the wagon. I got a little more shopping to do. This one is sort of a surprise for both of us."

She didn't question him. She started for the blacksmith's.

He found what he wanted at two stores, neighbor to each other on a side street. At one, he bought a little sack of red and white peppermint sticks, at the other two lemons. He took the nearest alley shortcut to the blacksmith shop.

This was the second-rate part of Peskar's business section, squalid, shabby. The alley, stinking with refuse and litter, paper, glass, garbage thrown from the back doors of the tumbledown shops which lined it went about a hundred feet, turned and entered a vacant lot set smack in its path. In the center of the vacant lot, among the dead fennel and ragweed, had been dumped three or four wagonloads of secondhand brick, a hot red in the noon sun now, flecked with gleaming white mortar. Three men were stretched supine on the bricks, as snakes bask in the sun, lethargically passing a whiskey bottle back and forth among them. When they saw Fugate, they arose and came forward, making a loose circle around him, about ten feet from him. The sun glare was ferocious. Fugate squinted at them.

They were all somewhere around twenty years old. Dregs, each of them. Fugate studied them with distaste; they looked as low down in the scale as humans could get. Two of them were wearing one-suspender bib overalls, and the other, in pants, rope belt, and dirty, pleated white shirt, collarless, was barefooted. Their grinning lips were pasty with wet chewing tobacco. "We caught us a hard case," said the barefooted one happily.

"Stand aside," said Fugate. "I'm coming through."

They didn't move.

"I'm giving y'all one more chance," said Fugate amiably. "Who are you, anyways?"

"Round town we're knowed as the Jackknife Boys," said the barefooted one. "They's three of us, and we always herd up this way."

They took jackknives from their pockets and did it like experts. All of the knives had sheep's foot points, beveled from the middle of the blood veined at the back of the blade to the tip. Two of them were stag-handled, one had a handle of home-whittled oak. They came out and open like fans, in a little easy movement.

"For your information," said Fugate patiently. "I don't play your game."

"We specialize on the likes of you," the barefoot one said. "Hard cases. They come into town hard cases and, when we finish with them, go out tame and like sausage meat."

Fugate asked, "What if I run?"

"We only hope you do."

"Then," said Fugate, "I guess I'm going to have to show you my pass. I didn't want to."

"They ain't no pass through us," said the barefoot man. The others waited, watching.

"Then how come you're personated," said Fugate. "How come it says "To Who it May Concern, especially The Jackknife Boys'?"

They looked amazed. "It couldn't say that," said the barefoot one.

"What do you think I got here?" asked Fugate. He took the rusty old razor from his hat. It looked mighty ugly in the sunlight.

They tightened, shocked.

"Peskar's a town of law and order," said the barefoot one. "You better not kill nobody here. They'll hang you."

"I wasn't aiming to kill nobody," said Fugate. "Y'all weren't aiming to kill me, were you?"

"No," said the barefoot one.

"Well, then that's all right," said Fugate.

The barefoot one said, "A single razor agin three knives? You don't stand a chance."

"I think so," said Fugate.

"We'll be all over you!"

"It's a risk I have to take," repeated Fugate.

They began to look disturbed. "What makes you so sure of yourself?" asked one of them in overalls.

"I fight my own style," said Fugate.

"And what would that be?" asked the same man.

Fugate explained, talking simply. "You got to cut to hurt. All I got to do is touch. You try to carve. I blind."

"You what?" Now the third one finally spoke.

Fugate said, "I fight eyes. The eyeball is a bladder filled with juice. All I got to do is brush it with a razor edge, and go on to the next man."

"That's a turrible way to fight," said the barefoot one, shaken.

"It always wins," said Fugate. "Let's get started. Why don't y'all try it with your knives? Of course, I've had more practice than y'all."

They gawked at him.

He said, "That's it. That's the secret. You just touch. A little touch. It's all in who is quickest with his little touches."

They suddenly looked lumpish and paralyzed.

Fugate said, "But if you think you wouldn't care for it, and if you think you'd rather go somewhere else, don't let me keep you."

They left at a stiff brisk walk.

He put the razor back in his hat.

His hand was shaking.

He'd dropped the two paper sacks when he'd first been confronted. Now he picked them up, put them in his shirt and rebuttoned it.

Back at the blacksmith's, he found that Amy, waiting on the wagon seat, had fed and curried the horses. He paid the smith, reclaimed his .38-40 and bowie and climbed up beside her. They drove off. A couple of miles out of town, he threw the razor into a clump of roadside sage. She smiled, "What was that?"

"Just a old broke razor," he said casually.

"In your hat?"

"I put it there so I wouldn't forget to throw it away," he explained.

"That doesn't make any sense to me," she said. "Does that make any sense to you?"

"No, ma'am," he said. "But each individual human has been foreordained. Don't you believe that?"

"Let's not talk for a while," she said. "Let's just ride and not say anything and enjoy ourselves."

Along about four o'clock, when the day was the hottest, he got out the peppermint sticks and the lemons. Carefully, but roughly, he rolled each of the lemons between his palms. "That's to mush 'em up a little inside," he said to her. Then, in their tops, he cut a deep cone with his bowie and jammed in a peppermint stick. He handed one to her, and kept the other himself. "Suck on it," he instructed.

She tried it. Warily. The elixir of the potent lemon juice, coming up through the peppermint candy, and flavored by it, was delicious beyond words.

"How you like it?" he asked.

She simply raised her eyebrows.

"It lasts, too," he said. "You'll see."

They settled back in the seat.

"I was taught to make one of these when I was eleven years old," he said.

With the setting of the sun, they came to a small square building, bright in wagon green paint, sitting flat on the flat prairie before a fork in some railroad tracks. Behind the building was a sorry-looking vegetable garden. It was a lonesome, desolate-looking landscape. "What's that?" asked Amy.

"A place called Cottonwood Junction," said Fugate. "We got to stop here a minute. I got to borrow some lucifers. We're getting dangerous low." They drove up to its front door.

Amy held the reins while he went inside.

A dowdy woman in silver-rimmed glasses and brown muslin dress was stuffing a veal breast. She had the meat on the bare counter and was ramming a pocket in it full of handfuls of corn bread dressing from a dishpan. A bald-headed man just behind her was sitting on a three-legged stool, reading a patent medicine almanac.

Fugate said, "My name is John Thomas Brown. I was expecting a telegram from Stinson County. Did it come in?"

"It did," said the man. He got up, took a paper from a wire hook and handed it over. "Six bits, seven cents," he said. Fugate paid him, walked a short distance toward the door, stopped and read it.

It said: *Dear friend stop there has been no Flying 8 here for some years stop it was purchased about four years ago by Eastern Seaboard Cattle a big syndicate in Philadelphia and at present is part of their holdings here in the county stop with the ESC brand stop there is no post office or store on it stop Kilburns Postoffice is a miserable little settlement over in the direction of the Washita River stop it is the name of a settlement not a man stop Charles Kilburn who founded it was killed by the Cheyennes back in the eighties.* (In the eighties. Before either Fugate or Amy were born.) *Just to oblige I have looked up your Foster Kilburn in births, deaths taxes etc. and can find absolutely no trace of any party by that name. Signed, Floyd McBride, County Clerk, Malloy, Stinson County, Oklahoma.*

Outside, Fugate mounted to the wagon seat.

Amy said, "The edges of your nostrils. They're snow white. Are you sick?"

"Just a little mad," he said. "They always get that way when I'm a little mad. It'll pass."

"Mad at what?"

"Let's get moving," he said. "Let's get on to Stinson County."

No ranch, no store, no Mr. Brockhaus, no Mr. Foster Kilburn, just fifteen thousand dollars in gold somehow gone up in smoke.

To get it back, to get part of it back even, the first thing was to find out exactly how they'd done it. How they'd tricked a smart old turtle like Mr. Dennis.

CHAPTER
SEVEN

Because they were on a road, if you could call ancient ruts and outcropping and grass tangled into rabbits' nests a road, and because they were warming toward their destination — only about a county and a half away, he told her — they drove all night, spelling each other at the reins.

Nine o'clock in the morning came, and the hot wind under the blazing brass sun seemed to dry the sweat on your wrists to crust. This was a country of red clay in low mounds, thirsty and harsh, nearly treeless, with swales of thin buffalo grass. Infrequently, there would be a stunted, twisted white oak. "You can kick and hammer a white oak to hell and gone," he said. "And it will just keep on growing." The water in the barrels turned tepid. He kept them carefully covered; they were just the right temperature for insect eggs. Just after breakfast, he had taken his Winchester from its boot and put it in the wagon, handy, just behind the seat. She'd asked why, and he'd said, "The meaner the country, the meaner the people."

"I thought you liked this kind of country," she'd said.
"I do," he'd answered. "When I'm somewheres else."
About ten they came to the building.

It was a long dilapidated structure, lonesome and abandoned looking, unpainted and silver tan from sand-blasting winds, roofed with hides and old tarpaulins and cast-off wagon sheets. To one side of it was a corral of rope and white oak posts. There was no one in sight. Sticking up from the roof ridge of the main building was a cottonwood plank, crudely lettered, saying: *MACCABEE, SR. & MACCABEE, JR. — Necessities, Sundries, & Feed*. Just beyond it, the road leading down to it and crossing it, was a wide, shallow stream, made up of red clay spits, sandstone rubble and discarded wagon gear, interspersed with barely flowing runlets. "The old Maccabee Ford," said Fugate. "We'd better go right by."

"You mean you don't trust these Maccabees?"

"There hasn't been a Maccabee here for years," said Fugate. "I don't know who is here now. Squatters of some kind. Probably bad ones."

"I'd like to look over their sundries," she said "I sure need a big-eye darning needle. One that I can thread up on the wagon seat here."

Exasperated, he said, "This is no store, I'm telling you!"

Three men came out of a door toward them.

One of them carried a seine, two poles with a split gunnysack between them, and a log chain along the bottom as the sinker. They were getting ready to seine the stream. And would probably eat anything they caught. Anything.

They were a repellent-looking trio. They were bristle faced, sly eyed and filthy. They stood in a knot at the

68

wagon's doubletree, and Fugate could smell stale urine and snuff. Amy said, "Mr. Maccabee, do you have any darning needles inside?" She spoke toward the group in general.

"Not as happens at the moment," said one of the men, flabby, stoop shouldered, with a flat caved in face. "But we expect some in on the next shipment."

"You *are* Mr. Maccabee, aren't you?" said Amy, pressing, trying to win a point over Fugate.

"Mr. Maccabee is out at present," said the man.

"And been out for six years, the way I hear it," said Fugate. "Who are you?"

"Mr. Lovelace," said the flabby man. "And these other gentlemen aside me, being of no kin to me, naturally go by other names."

All at once, Fugate realized something.

They had a seine, all right, and seemed all set for the stream, but where were they going to put their catch — those little turtles, and fish, and frogs, and all that underwater stuff they were going to bring home.

Nowhere. They had no sack nor bag, nor even basket.

The answer was that they weren't going seining. They were just pretending. They had come out to take a good look at Amy and Fugate and the wagon.

"Where you'uns headed?" asked Mr. Lovelace.

"None of yore goddam business," said Fugate. "If the lady will excuse the expression."

"I've been knowed to use it myself," said Amy. "You gentlemen just go ahead and talk and don't mind me."

The three squatters turned, walked back to the building and went inside again.

Fugate snipped the reins, said, "Yup!" to the team, and the wagon moved on. "Looks like you're my hired gun after all," said Amy.

"Don't you believe it," he retorted.

In a businesslike way, she said, "You'll get your wages after the first cattle sale."

"I can hardly wait," he said seriously.

They were maybe fifteen minutes gone from Maccabee's Ford, when Fugate said, "Well, there it is."

"What?" she asked.

"Our hill," he said. "Right ahead. Here's where we wait for them."

It was sort of a double hill, two mounds of red clay, their slopes covered with brush and scrub and runty oaks, the road passing between them. "What are we doing?" she asked.

"You'll see," he said. "And I got an idea we better work fast."

They drove the wagon behind the right-hand hill, stopped at the edge of a gully and got down. Rapidly he tied the team to a sapling. "Take my mare," he said crisply. "And go up to that thicket yonder." He pointed to the crest of the hill on the left. "Hide. If this doesn't work out, ride like hell."

"For where?" she asked.

"For Kansas."

"Are you going to be in trouble?"

"Yes, ma'am."

"Then I'll stay here and help," she said firmly.

"No, ma'am," he said. "When I'm in trouble, I like plenty of elbowroom."

She unhitched his mare from the tailgate and mounted. "How can you be so sure?" she asked skeptically.

He was examining his rifle, throwing a shell into the chamber. "Back at Maccabee's Ford," he said. "The ground had been fresh swept by the hitching rail. A horse had just been there. They'd seen us coming and got it out of the way in a hurry. And messed up its tracks."

"I don't believe it," she said. "Where did it go?"

"There was a new path swept to the door. You don't sweep bare earth, you know, Miss Amy."

"You mean it was in the house!"

"I'd say so. With somebody probably holding its muzzle so it wouldn't neigh. They didn't want bloodshed there."

"Who?"

"Who do you think? I'd say that Dave Lawson. That's where he'd wait. At a ford. Now get!"

She rode up the hillside and vanished.

His voice had sounded granular and raspy, and he knew it and was ashamed of it.

He started up his hill. There was broken shade, but the vines made tough going, and the tree roots were twisted and gnarled and treacherous, sometimes looping up above the eroded clay. It had been an extra hot summer, and everything was sere and tinder dry. Because of the brush, he couldn't see six feet ahead of him or six feet behind him. He saw no birds, no rabbits, and listened constantly for that sinister little rattle, tinny and shell-like, but heard nothing. Nothing but his own steps. Walking as carefully as he could, he couldn't keep from swishing the dead curled oak leaves on the ground. You could walk through pines without a whisper and through black gum, but no one, not even a Comanche, could move silently through crisp old oak leaves.

When he reached the hilltop, he looked around, judged pros and cons, picked the right place and stretched out.

There were trees over him but none before him. He lay stretched out full-length on his stomach, in the mast and leaves, in the half-rotted twigs and acorns, his rifle before him, resting in the cleft between two gray lichen-covered rocks. He could see the road below plainly. Across from him, he could see the facing hilltop. He searched it carefully with his gaze and couldn't see Amy. Brush, saplings, undergrowth, yes. But not Amy. That was the way he wanted it.

They came into view below him suddenly. And stopped in the middle of the road, in the crotch between the hills, directly beneath him. There were four of them; Dave Lawson and the three squatters from the ford.

Lawson was talking, gesturing to the others. Laying down commands. It was a good picture of a boss with three temporary helpers. He'd probably paid them a pittance just to come along and help handle anything that came up. But they had guns, could shoot and would. And they'd go whole hog in case of trouble, there was no doubt of that.

One of the squatters — Mr. Lovelace — disengaged himself from the others and disappeared down the road. Scouting.

He returned, rejoining the others, and again they put their heads together. Consulting. He was reporting the empty wagon.

The men studied the hillsides, first Fugate's, then Amy's.

They held another discussion, came to a decision and got moving. They dismounted, divided into two groups, and started up the slopes. Two of the squatters started up Amy's hill, Lawson and Mr. Lovelace began to climb Fugate's hill.

He watched them moodily. He had a feeling he could have picked them all off rapid fire, as they sat their horses there in the road, though it would have taken top-notch, hawk eye shooting. And it would have been slaughter. That chance was now gone.

The thing, no matter what, was to get those two away from Amy and bring them all to him.

He scraped up a little pile of leaves and twigs, lit it, got it going and put on some grass. A finger of thick smoke went up from it in the hot air, smudgy, gray black.

Down below they started to yell. Lawson bawled, "They're up here! You men come over!"

The two squatters from Amy's hill came racing down their slope and dashing up Fugate's. Then, from Amy's hilltop rose a column of smoke.

She'd started her own counter fire to bring them back. To help Fugate.

He looked at it furiously.

Lovelace called, "One back yonder now, too. What the hell is this?"

Lawson yelled, "Forget the second one! Let's all work together on this one. We'll clean 'em out one at a time!"

"I'm afeared it's some kind of signal they got atwixt them!" yelled Mr. Lovelace.

"Don't bother about signals, just climb this hill!" called Lawson.

Fugate made a quick change of strategy. They would be expecting him to be doing this very thing, to be holed up on the hilltop. All they'd have to do would be surround him, and hem him in, and then it would simply be a question of time. He'd better be in a position where he could shift his ground.

If he could get down through them, somehow, and come up behind them, he might nail two before they knew what was what. And that would alter the odds considerably. He rushed down the slope.

He took about eight lunging steps, for time was a critical element, and went through a mat of dead brush and leaves into a hidden arroyo. Its red clay sides were gouged and groved with centuries of rains, and grass tufts and scrub overhung its rims. Its floor, a couple of feet wide, was of sun-caked red clay silt. Fugate held his rifle across his breast, bent over and, at a gentle running pace, loped down its grade.

All at once there was a crook in it, and all at once three panting men stood before him. The squatters from Maccabee's Ford.

Fugate, keeping his Winchester across his chest, not even bringing it into firing position, said steadily, "Well, it's up to you. You want to take a try at it or not?"

"No," said Mr. Lovelace, showing wild panic. "And I speak for all of us."

"Drop your gun belts," said Fugate.

They did, very carefully.

Men like this had a life to live. They saw no sense in an open contest.

"I got a wife and three children in Texas," said Mr. Lovelace. "And we're all honest men, don't we look it?"

"All you look to me," said Fugate, "is three coyote-eat skeletons rotting away in an Oklahoma canyon."

"Don't talk that way, don't talk that way," said Mr. Lovelace.

"I'm just speaking my mind," said Fugate tonelessly.

"I know you are," said Mr. Lovelace. "I know you are. Don't take it I'm arguing with you."

A new voice came down into the arroyo. Dave Lawson's voice. It said, "Let your gun fall, son. It's all over. Where is the girl?"

It was the "where is the girl" part, the fact that it was really Amy he was after, that got Lawson killed. He should have shot Fugate on sight, but he had to know about Amy first.

Fugate turned his head. Lawson was thrust out — head, shoulders, fists and gun — over the arroyo's rim above him. He was about nine feet up.

Fugate shot him in the matted hair of his left eyebrow. He swung his rifle around and up — a lot like a man would take a slash at a fly — and touched off the trigger as the gun sight passed its target. Lawson came crashing over the edge, dead, all arms and legs, Fugate shot him again, with care, as you'd shoot a bear tumbling at you from a mountain ledge. Mr. Lovelace and his friends stood frozen stiff.

Lawson's body lay on the clay and sandstone shards of the arroyo bed. His pouched leathery face sagged now, and tight leather chaps and gray shirt seemed somehow all mussed up together. "A nameless skeleton, forgot, on a Oklahoma canyon bed," murmured Mr. Lovelace.

Fugate spoke to the dead man. In a voice of velvet, he said, "Girl mauler."

There was a moment of utter silence.

Then Mr. Lovelace, dry mouthed, asked, "What's going to happen to us?"

"We'll see," said Fugate. "Why did he bring you along?"

"Just to help out in a general way, he said," answered Mr. Lovelace.

"Help out at what?" asked Fugate.

"Teaching you'uns a lesson for stealing his wagon. Giving the both of you a big spook so you wouldn't never do nothing like that again," said Mr. Lovelace. "Nothing serious."

Fugate asked, "How much blood money did he pay you?"

"It wasn't supposed to be blood money," said Mr. Lovelace. "And he didn't pay us nothing. He was to pay us when it was all over."

"Well, it's all over," said Fugate. "I'm leaving. You can take your pay off him after I've gone. If you want to."

"We don't want to," said Mr. Lovelace desperately. "All we want is to get gone, too."

Fugate found Amy on her hilltop without too much trouble and said, "Dave Lawson isn't going to give us any more trouble, he promised."

She looked doubtful, and said, "But a man like that. Would you take his promise?"

"Yes," said Fugate. "And so would you. You should have seen him. He wet his fingertip and crossed his heart and even took out a little pocket testament and swore a oath."

She looked impressed. "That sounds okay," she said. "What was the shooting I heard?"

"I didn't hear any shots," he said, relaxed. "Maybe you were just a little nervous."

"What became of the other three? The squatters from the ford?"

"Oh them," said Fugate. "Them and me became good friends. Mr. Lovelace has a wife and three children in Texas. Did you know that?"

"No, I didn't," she said. They went down the wooded slope to the wagon. As she climbed onto the seat, she said, "What was a man like that Lawson man doing carrying around a testament? You said he swore on a testament."

Fugate seated himself beside her and picked up the reins. "It wasn't exactly a testament," he said. "It was a sack of Bull Durham. It was the best he could do, but his heart was in it."

"In Kansas —" she started.

"I know," he said. "Back in Kansas they do it different."

CHAPTER
EIGHT

The pike, which since Cottonwood Junction had swerved from the railroad track, now met it again, rejoined it and ran parallel to it, west, in the direction in which they were traveling. It was dusty and scorching, and their wagon wheels left a churned fog of dust along the road behind them. They passed few travelers. At intervals, though, they passed track-side chutes and stock pens. What cattle they could see from the road looked well fatted. It was lonesome country — endless blue gray grass and cloudless, searing sky — but there were people here, you could feel it.

Fugate said, "We're in Stinson County. Malloy, the county seat, is about fourteen miles further on. It might be a good idea to figure to get there tomorrow morning. How are you making out?"

"I'm fine," she said. "And I'm sure glad it's all over."

He was careful not to look at her. He said, "We been passing some mighty good cows, some mighty good suet."

A little later, he said, "We're due to come into a village soon, if you can call about four houses a village. Name of Sheep Jaw."

"Sheep Jaw?" she said.

"Named for a man," explained Fugate. "Sheep Jaw Erickson."

"It's a disgusting name," she said.

"He was a disgusting man," said Fugate.

The place, when they drove into it, seemed at first to Amy all stock pens and loading chutes. It was a minor shipping point for this end of the county, he told her. She asked if *Flying 8* shipped here and he said no, that *Flying 8* shipped at Malloy.

Only two of the four buildings were houses. Of the other two, one was a saloon and general store, the other, on a little square of pine planking by the tracks, was the railroad shipping and passenger office. The buildings, their foundations fringed with tall weeds, were in a short strip between the tracks and the pike. The heat was fiery. The soft dust beneath their wagon rims was like thick tan flour. The women were under the cool of their roofs probably, Fugate decided.

A man in a baize coat came out of the back door of the railroad office, and yelled, "You the Dennis folks?" at them.

"Yes," called Amy. "No," called Fugate.

The man came forward. "I was supposed to keep a eye peeled for you all," he said. "Wagon, team of dapples, and all. And stop you. Here it is. Your telegram."

He handed a paper to Fugate.

Fugate read it. It said: *I and the hands at Flying 8 are eagerly awaiting your arrival and take-over stop a slight difficulty has come up in the legal end though stop would like to talk over this unimportant point with you*

80

stop I will meet you and explain at a place called The Osages stop The Osages is a deserted ranch house with an old windmill in a clump of osage bushes on your way about five miles west of Sheep Jaw stop just pull in and wait stop I hope to show up about midnight. Signed Foster Kilburn.

Foster Kilburn again.

Fugate handed the telegram to Amy.

She read and nodded. "That's more like it," she said. "Finally we're going to get this thing straightened out."

"Was the telegram sent from Malloy?" Fugate asked the man.

"Right," said the man.

"This is nice country," said Amy. "Why would a ranch house like that be deserted, and with a windmill and all?"

"Rancher that lived there had a vision in his sleep one night," said the railroad man. "It come to him in a dream that a new ax he'd just bought was a sham with a tissue paper blade. He jumped up and tried it out on his wife and young'uns. Nobody relished moving in sinst."

Amy said weakly, "My!"

"That ain't no kind of tale to tell before a lady," said Fugate patiently.

Bridling, the man said, "I wear a Purity, Honor, and Fellowship button that I won when I was six years old. I don't drink, don't smoke, and gotta always tell the truth."

"You look mighty serious," said Amy to Fugate. "Is something worrying you?"

"No," said Fugate. "What could there be?"

He was thinking about that hot breath still so close to their trail. Here in Sheep Jaw, even.

At first it seemed ghostly, and then it began to make sense. There was only one road into Malloy from the east, really, this road. "Foster Kilburn" had laid this last trap for them as a final safety precaution, automatically, if everything else should fail him.

Fugate, speaking to the railroad man, said, "What's the man's address, the man that sent this?"

"I don't know, and if I did know, I wouldn't tell you."

"You were paid a little something extra, weren't you," said Fugate, "to watch for us and deliver it?"

"That's none of your affair."

"How long have you been watching?" asked Fugate.

"Three days."

"Are you an errand boy for the railroad or for this Foster Kilburn?"

"I never heard of Mr. Kilburn before. And I don't take your conversation kindly."

"Once more. What's his Malloy address?"

The railroad man simply shook his head.

Fugate said, "You're going back to your key right now and telegraph him. And the telegram is going to say: *Mr. Kilburn, I delivered your message.*"

"What makes you so sure?"

"Or how is he going to get out to The Osages and meet us?"

"Well, what if I am?"

Speaking in a funereal voice, Fugate said, "You know what you're messing in?"

The man looked nervous. "What?"

"Kilburn is a white slaver from up north. He's trying to get his clutches on Miss Amy, here, and peddle her for a few pieces of evil silver."

"Mr. Fugate!" exclaimed Amy. "This is too much!"

"*And*," said Fugate, "Miss Amy's got some hot-tempered friends. You're going to hear hoofbeats in the middle of some lonesome night."

"The name is Foster Kilburn, Pagett House, Malloy," said the man. "To satisfy my own curiosity, are you Mr. Dennis?"

"I'm a Mr. Dennis," said Fugate. "They's dozens of us."

"I'll forget you, if you forget me," said the man. "Shall I send the telegram?"

"Sure," said Fugate. "Why not?"

"He's hard to understand, isn't he?" said Amy to the man.

The man turned and headed back to the building. Fugate and Amy called, "Good day!" to his retreating back.

"Wait here," said Fugate. He got down, went across the road and entered the saloon, next to the depot.

Inside, it was the kind of saloon you'd see in any small cattle shipping point, off season.

The room was tinder dry, lye scrubbed and bare. Three men, villagers, constant habitués Fugate decided, sat together at a little table just within the door. Avoiding honest work, avoiding wives. Across the room, facing the door, was the bar, with a chubby aproned man behind it, swabbing the bar-top with a chamois. Fugate went to the bar and said, "Four roast beef sandwiches." He laid down two dimes; the sandwiches would be a nickle apiece. Roast beef sandwiches were drinkers standbys; most saloons sold them. This one did.

The barman took the meat and a loaf of bread from beneath the counter and began to slice. When he had finished, he laid out catsup, mustard, horseradish and a bowl of chopped sweet pickle. The three villagers tired of catching flies, tired of sitting staring at each other, came up to the bar.

"These here are Mr. Haglemeyer, Mr. Marstonbury, and Mr. Sandrow," said the barman, making a party of it, introducing them gallantly.

"Pleased to meet you," said Fugate politely. Then, introducing himself, he said, "I'm Sac River Jones."

"Doing a little traveling, Mr. Jones?" asked Mr. Sandrow.

"That's right," said Fugate.

"Come from a distance?" asked Mr. Haglemeyer.

"A distance," agreed Fugate.

"And headed for a distance," said Mr. Marstonbury.

"That's right," said Fugate. He picked up the sandwiches, two in each hand, said adios and left. Living in Sheep Jaw must be worse than living in hell, he thought.

He and Amy ate the sandwiches in the thin scorching shade of the wagon, sitting haunched up on their heels in the red clay-dust. She said, "What a nice little town!

Washings on every line. Wives busy as all get out, carrying buckets of water from wells, beating rugs, washing windows, even one yonder up on a roof, hammering. It makes me homesick."

"If you're through," said Fugate, "let's get on our way." They eached downed a dipper of water from one of the barrels and climbed up onto the seat.

He said, "They're figuring on a trap for us at that old ranch house. Shall we sidestep it, or shall we see what's what?"

"Let's see what's what," she said.

He patted her on the top of her head with the flat of his hand. Gently, as you would pat a dog. "Good girl," he said. She squeezed tight her eyes and pulled in her lips with pleasure. He started the team, and they left Sheep Jaw.

They could see the rusty, broken old windmill before the pike came alongside of it. For a mile the roadside had been giant matted osage and suddenly they came to a narrow wagon lane turning directly into the matted denseness. Fugate guided the team from the pike into the lane. He'd seen osage thickets without count throughout his life, but he'd never seen one as impenetrable and interlaced as this one. He didn't see or hear any birds either, and birds like brush and thickets. The lane was strewn with putrid, scattered mock oranges. He tried not to think of the rancher who had ax-killed his family back in here. Abruptly the lane came out into the open, and they were in the old ranch yard.

There was the house, about forty feet away, two stories, its siding already paint blistered and cupped, showing rusty nails half sprung from the joists. Behind the house were the outbuildings, barn and open forge and sheds, tumbledown and overgrown with wiry pineweed, called by some orange grass. Fugate and Amy got down. He watered and fed the team of dapples, combed them a little, then reharnessed them and hitched them to a ringbolt on an oak post set in the parched earth a few yards away. It was about four in the afternoon.

"We'll eat now," he said.

"But it's early," she said. "And we've got plenty of time."

"How do you know we got plenty of time?" he said. "These here are sly ones." They ate.

When they had eaten, they explored the house, Fugate with gun in hand.

They entered a dusty parlor, and that meant that before the rancher had got his bad dream about the ax the ranch was beginning to prosper, because few folks in the out country had parlors; kitchens, actually, were parlors. They went upstairs, looked into stark furnitureless bedrooms, descended, examined the downstairs rooms and came into the kitchen. The empty house gave Fugate a strange feeling. For one thing, a house is never empty, really. People leave, but other things move in: mice, rats, moths and spiders. People have a smell, but these things have their smell, too.

Suddenly the kitchen had a people smell to him, a smell of cooking. It was faint and not exactly recent, but it was there. He glanced around. It was like any medium prosperous ranch house kitchen. Pine cupboards, golden varnished, now dingy and streaked. A zinc sink with a cast iron pump and pump handle. Bare floor, cobwebbed ceiling, no table, no chairs, no range. Rat droppings on the floor along the baseboard. There was a stovepipe up, though looking pretty makeshift, and at its base was a small, broken-down, secondhand cannonball stove. With a skillet and a coffeepot on it. Fugate went to the cupboard above the sink and opened it.

Before him, on the shelf, just above eye level, was a barn lantern, a can of coffee, a canister of cornmeal, a hunk of something wrapped in oily paper which proved to be rock hard dried beef, and a neatly stacked pile of cardboard boxes of rifle cartridges. Fugate took down a box, opened it, took out a cartridge and looked at it. It was a rimmed .30, a Krag. Amy, looking over his shoulder, said, "Steel-jacket."

"That's right," said Fugate. "Our old friend again. Though, o' course, as a schoolteacher once explained to me, you're calling it wrong to call it steel. They's a lead plug in the middle, and the outside coating is a mixture of copper and nickle. It just looks like steel. Steel would gut your barrel." Thoughtfully, he replaced the box and shut the cupboard door.

Dave Lawson and his two friends, the man in the striped coat and the man with the Krag, the one with the bandolier; this is where they had worked from. This had been their headquarters, near to Malloy, near to Foster Kilburn. It was a good hideout.

"Let's go to the barn," said Fugate. "And stop by the wagon."

At the wagon they got Fugate's rifle and Amy's handgun.

The barn was a little behind the house but to the left of it. They went in, climbed a slat ladder nailed to the wall and came up into the loft. Fugate opened the loft door about six inches. They could see partly past the front corner of the house, see the wagon plainly and the team. "Lie down," said Fugate. They stretched out on the rough loft floor, their faces together at the crack. On the sill in front of him, Fugate laid out his rifle, his .38-40 Colt, and the old .44 revolver Amy had been flourishing back on the plain, during the attack when her father had been killed.

"I figure we got a pretty long wait," Fugate said. "Why don't you loosen up a little and take a snooze."

She rolled over on her shoulder and was almost instantly asleep.

The sun set; then there was a mustard-colored afterglow, and dusk. Dusk and night became one. The late moon was just showing itself in shredded clouds — which, according to Fugate's calculations, would make it about ten o'clock, not twelve — when a man walked through the moonlit ranch yard toward the wagon.

As he came, he called, "I'm a friend, a friend!"

Fugate touched his rifle and lifted it quietly. The movement awakened Amy. He put his finger up and down across her lips for silence.

Down below, in the ranch yard, the man put his head into the wagon, called, "Hello, hello," stood a minute and went into the dark house. After an interval, they saw yellow in the kitchen window. The yellow moved from room to room, upstairs, downstairs.

The man came out with the lighted barn lantern and looked inside the wagon.

"Long gone," he said distinctly.

He put the lantern out, set it on the ground and unhitched the team. He got onto the wagon seat and drove off. Down the lane, as they had come.

Amy scrambled half erect in pursuit. Fugate grabbed her. "Hold it," he whispered. "That's bait. You didn't see his horse, did you? He had to have a horse. Steady."

They waited perhaps ten minutes. A second man came into the ranch yard, riding, a saddled horse in lead. "That one was laying back in the shadows to kill us," said Fugate. "Unless I'm wrong, that one is Foster Kilburn."

You could just make out the mounted man, you couldn't make out anything about him. He stared at the dark blank house and rode down the lane.

"We'll give them another hour," said Fugate.

Desperately, she said, "Gone. My wagon, my team, our food. Your horse."

He said, "But we're alive."

They climbed down the loft ladder, went out into the moonlight of the ranch yard and started through the pitch blackness of the lane.

After a bit, they reached the pike.

Mallory, Fugate figured, must be about nine miles ahead.

Amy said, "If the first man took the wagon just to draw us out in the open for the second man, like you said, they probably won't take it far. Is that right?"

"Could very well be," answered Fugate. "So don't let's pass it in the dark."

Suddenly, about an hour later, they left the black swathing of the osage bushes behind them and were out again into the moonlight.

A little farther on, they saw something whitish scattered along the right hand roadside, and heard the amiable snort of a horse. "That's Honeybee, my off dapple," said Amy. "Speaking to me."

They stopped. Fugate whipped a lucifer across the seat of his pants and held the bubble of sulphur flame aloft.

There were the horses, Fugate's and Amy's, and the wagon. In a little turfy clearing. The horses were untouched, Fugate saw instantly. But they'd sure played hell with the wagon. Amy had said it had been searched before, but that searching must have been nothing compared to this searching. The wagon bed was bare and empty. Everything movable, food, papers, clothes, tools, utensils, rope and spare harness had been taken out, probably examined, and thrown helter-skelter on the earth. And thrown angrily from the looks of it. The very wildness of it all frightened Amy.

"I should have give it to him from the loft," said Fugate calmly.

They found two candles in the litter, lighted them and began restoring and replacing things. It was a slow and tedious job, for the wagon to Amy was the same as a house, and there was a particular place for each thing, and no place else would do. They finished in the wash of a scarlet dawn.

"They must have been looking for something pretty small," said Amy. "I can't think what it could be. I guess they think now that we have it on us."

"Do you?" asked Fugate. "Think we have it on us?"

They mounted the wagon seat.

"Do you?" said Fugate.

"No," said Amy, nettled.

The wheels creaked and squeaked.

CHAPTER
NINE

The town of Malloy, seat of Stinson County, looked exactly what it was: ninety-three percent cattle, seven percent predators, badmen and short-card players. It was still before noon when Fugate and Amy drove their wagon along Main Street. The oven dryness of pounding sun had withered and shrunk the unseasoned planking and timbers of the buildings, and the rolling plains winds from up Beaver County way had left little corners of dust in office and shop windows. A continuous hitching rail ran down the two center blocks of Main Street, but, as in each case it was erected and paid for by the merchant it fronted, it varied greatly; some places it was a chain, some places a quarter-oak six-by-six, some places a peeled pole. Though it was near the noontime dinner hour, the sacred hour of hours, the slab pine walk seemed fairly busy. "Malloy's a burg with money," said Fugate.

"And I know where they spend it," said Amy. "Look at the saloons! Like flies on a ham bone."

Fugate pulled up at a rack before a building with a sign saying, *Padgett House*. It had a tin roof, with ridgelike seams, a double veranda, upstairs and downstairs in front, and its patch-painted siding looked like scrap lumber from some old dance hall. But you couldn't tell in small towns, Fugate knew; it could be the most dignified and respected hotel in three counties. He got down from the seat and handed Amy the reins. "Are we going to stay here?" she asked. "Shall I drive to some livery and leave the wagon and horses?"

"I don't know yet where we're staying," he said. "Because I don't know how long this is going to take. But likely not here. We're not too well fixed for do-re-mi, and these town hotels are cash crazy. Drive around and wait for me in front of the courthouse."

"The courthouse!"

"Yes, ma'am." He touched his hat politely and went inside.

Inside, to his surprise, the lobby turned out to be a sort of collection of little offices. There was the hotel desk, of course, with its ledger and clerk to his left, but in the back right-hand corner was a wicket with a sign saying RANCHERS EXPRESS. In the front right-hand corner, catercorner, was a little counter with a sign behind it saying, Oxford & Johnson, L. K. & N. Mockingbird, Mead Bros. These latter, Fugate knew, were small independent stage lines, sprouting off into the back country, making railroad connections elsewhere. The hotel clerk, whoever he happened to be at the moment, would be the agent for the whole caboodle.

Fugate went to the hotel counter. The present clerk behind it was jowl jawed, mean eyed, with a lumpy, red-veined nose. He looked Fugate up and down, and said, "If you're in the mind to buy a bath, we don't sell them here. You'll have to buy one at a barbershop somewhere."

Fugate said quietly, "My name is Kettingham. When people speak to me, they call me Mr. Kettingham."

"Or what?" said the clerk.

"Or I find myself in a sheriff's office explaining," said Fugate.

"Yes, Mr. Kettingham," said the clerk. "How can I help you?"

"I'd like a word with Mr. Foster Kilburn," said Fugate.

"Foster Kilburn?" said the man. "I don't recall nobody of that cognomen. He don't put up here. What is his appearance?"

"Just ordinary," said Fugate. "You on duty here yesterday afternoon or night?" asked Fugate.

"Long swing yesterday," said the man. "Day *and* night."

Then he'd delivered the Sheep Jaw telegram to Kilburn. He was lying through his teeth, but that didn't mean necessarily that he was involved. A caution would keep him mum.

"Do you think Mr. Kilburn might come in?" asked Fugate.

"How do I know who'll come in? This place is the crossroad of the universe."

"If you see him, would you tell him I have been here? Albert Kettingham."

"Sure. Or you could leave a note," said the clerk. "I got a box of notes and letters and such under the

94

counter. Folks leave 'em for other folks. Cowboys, drummers, ranchers, everybody."

"No note," said Fugate. "Just a word of mouth message. Tell him that Louisiana is back in the Union."

That should mix him up. That ought to mess up the trail.

"Louisiana back in the Union?" said the clerk, slack jawed. "That's been knowed for years, Mr. Kettingham."

"Just tell him," said Fugate.

He nodded and left.

They had passed the courthouse on their way down Main. It was one of three buildings set close together in a line, with a vacant lot at each end and a sort of public corral behind them. The first building, one story, about a three roomer with siding that ran up and down and with a T-shaped tile chimney, Fugate figured to be the town hall. The second, of brick, squat and grubby looking with barred windows, would be the jail. The courthouse was last in the line and the largest. Its entrance had double doors. It was two storied like the Padgett House, was tin roofed like the Padgett House, and had an upstairs-downstairs set of porches like the Padgett House. That's how the county funds had vaunted themselves, Fugate thought, in a sorry imitation Padgett House. He passed by Amy and the wagon at the curb, tipped his hat to her — by lifting it straight upward about eight inches; a gentleman always really *uncovers* to a lady on the street, never just pretends to, he'd been told — said, "Wait," and went through the courthouse doors.

He looked around, climbed stairs to a door marked County Clerk and entered. A little bald-headed man with home-mended spectacles was on his knees with another man over a red setter, lying belly up on the floor, inspecting it.

The men stood up. The setter got to its feet. Fugate asked, "Can I find Mr. Floyd McBride in here?"

"I'm Mr. McBride," said the bald-headed man pleasantly.

"They tell me you know the county pretty well," said Fugate.

"Between the two of us, maybe we do," said McBride. "Leave me make you knowed to my cousin, Sheriff McBride."

Fugate looked at the sheriff, and the sheriff met his gaze amiably. Stringy, elderly, threadbare, with genial eyes like charcoal marks on buckskin, he was the kind of old-timer Fugate respected instantly. There was wisdom in this man, and vast experience and humanity. Fugate said, "My name is Joe Fugate. I'm with a young pilgrim outside name of Miss Amy Dennis. We want to now the best and quickest way to get to a back-country settlement knowed as Kilburns Postoffice, somewhere's near the Washita River."

County Clerk McBride told him, briefly and clearly, naming landmarks.

Fugate said, "Free passage all the way? No buck-shotting trespassers?"

"You'll go through *Flying 8* country," said the county clerk. "But that's Eastern Seaboard Cattle now, and they buckshot."

"What's Eastern Seaboard Cattle?" asked Fugate.

"A Philadelphia syndicate," said the county clerk. "That's all the rage back there on the Atlantic coast now. Buying up Oklahoma land and making cow factories out of them. Mighty good people, though. And they tolerate old-timers such as me and the sheriff here."

Sheriff McBride got into the conversation. He said, "Mind if I ask you a question, son?"

"Of course not," Fugate replied.

Seriously, the sheriff said, "You ain't come to Stinson County to slay and maim, have you?"

"No," said Fugate.

"Because you're a catgut fiddle string," said the sheriff. "I look at you and see myself at your age. But I was decent, I was decent. You decent?"

"Yes, sir," said Fugate.

"Have a good trip," said the sheriff. "And I only hope nobody misjudges you. For their sake."

Fugate jerked his chin courteously to each of them, half raised his hand in a gesture and departed.

Down at the curb, Amy was glad to see him. He took his place at the driver's end of the seat and tucked the reins into his palm. She said, "What happened? What did you do in there? What do we do now?"

"We go to Kilburns Postoffice," he said. "The real and only one. It's a settlement. There's nothing at the *Flying 8* like a post office or a store either, I'd say."

She took it pretty well. After a moment, she said, "What about the *Flying 8* itself? Is there a *Flying 8*?"

"Seems like no," he said. "We're going to look into that, too."

In a perfectly steady voice, she said, "I go back to Kansas. Is that it?"

"How do I know?" he said desperately. "I ain't King Solomon."

"But you've got an idea of some kind. Mr. Fugate always has some kind of idea."

"Yes, ma'am, I have."

"Would you care to let me in on it?"

"It's that I get your money back. So you can buy yourself a ranch as good, or maybe even better than the *Flying 8*."

Beads gathered on her eyelashes, and she seemed to be crying inwardly.

He said, "Well, you asked me!"

The sun ran down to the choking twilight. Beyond a low mesa — one of Sheriff McBride's landmarks — Fugate handed the reins to Amy. "I'll be back," he said. He saddled his pony. There was grass, grass and grass, west, east, north, south. He rode along the path of the butte face, passed a shoulder of rock, passed a notice on a gate, Eastern Seaboard Cattle Company, came to buildings and hitched. He entered an office. A man sat by a desk beyond a railing, near a window.

Fugate said, "Evening."

The man was barbered, coatless, a vest with a double row of buttons — citified. On the desk top were his cuffs, his starched collar, tie and garnet tiepin. He was writing. He lay down the pen.

"I'm Mr. Brace, the manager," he said. "Can I help?"
Fugate looked around.

The walls were white painted, the floor was stained oak, the furniture was veneered, glossy and new. Eastern Seaboard was high-toned, Fugate thought. Classy. Through the window, Fugate saw horses, trappings, gear and shadowy men. Fugate said, "I lost my trail. Where am I?"

"That rock out there is Yellow Mesa," said Mr. Brace.

"I'm trying to find a place name of Kilburns Postoffice."

"You are now west of the Washita River," said Mr. Brace. "And about fifteen miles north."

A cowboy rolled through the door, leather, tan cotton and buckles. Hard-bitten. Bowlegged. Tough.

Toeing, thought Fugate, almost. Some men walk that way.

"Mr. Brace, sir," said the hand. "The cook wants you to send a team to Malloy in the morning. Some blackjack molasses, lard and saleratus, Mr. Brace, sir."

Mr. Brace, sir, Mr. Brace, sir, thought Fugate sourly. Eastern Seaboard manners.

"Very well, Dixie," said Mr. Brace.

The cowboy departed.

"Wayfaring?" said Mr. Brace.

"Yes."

"Where do you come from?" asked Mr. Brace.

"Hard to say."

Mr. Brace riffled into his letters. Fugate passed through the doorway.

★ ★ ★

A few steps away Dixie, the cowboy, held a horse at a galvanized watering vat. Fugate came over. The horse was powerful, with a coppery coat and a silvery roached mane. Fugate said, "Good looking churn-head."

Dixie went on with his business.

"Is this your horse?" said Fugate.

"Stand back, sport," said Dixie. "Dust off."

Fugate stood patiently.

"It's Mr. Brace's horse," said Dixie. "The boss. Mr. Brace likes show-style city horses. Roached."

"Roached," said Fugate. "My goodness. A horse with bay rum and with a haircut?" he said rapturously.

"We don't like floaters," said Dixie harshly.

Fugate said, "I'm no floater."

The cowboy led the horse away.

Fugate mounted his pony.

Amy was behind the mesa, in the dark. Fugate settled down beside her. Night noises, murmurs, came across the prairie. The wagon pitched and swayed through the desiccated bugleweeds. Fugate meditated. Amy glanced at him and away.

Later she said, "Sleeping?"

They had about talked themselves out.

"I'm not sleeping," he said. "I am cogitating."

She curled warmly on his shoulder.

A tatter of Fugate's memory nagged him. Three years last October, he had crossed Caddo County. One broiling day he had turned a winding, stony wash and come upon a shack on timber stilts, a store, a cross-trails' rendezvous. A storekeeper had leaned on the open door. Before it, a thickset steamy-faced cowhand held a smoking Smith & Wesson. A downy cheeked plowboy lay dead, collapsed, his tinny revolver in his holster. Fugate and his pony had ambled up, easy gaited. The cowboy had shouted, "He was fixing to draw on me!" Fugate had looked straight ahead.

It was the cowboy from the store, three years ago in the wash.

Dixie.

CHAPTER
TEN

The midnight sky was curdled, overcast. They left the grasslands, drove through sparse belts of pines and flat and boulders and paper thin soil. "Kilburn Postoffice, coming up," said Fugate. They came to a place where a cabin and a stable with an open-faced blacksmith's shed stood dark and formless. They alighted; he hitched. She stood beside him. He knocked and called. A man with lantern and a rifle, said, "Come in, folks." Unshaven, he wore dirty pants and nothing else.

The man stepped back and they entered. He hung his lantern at a thong from a roof beam.

"Pope Gurley," he introduced. "Proprietor and hermit."

Fugate said, "Where's Globe?"

"Globe is in Arizona, sonny. You're mixed up. It's Arizona. You go through a corner of Texas to get there." He hesitated. "And clean through New Mexico."

The cabin was small and very old and grubby. With bugs, mice, snakes, and spiders, Fugate supposed. Odors of collards and urine and bacon grease. Bolted behind them was the door. On their right was an iron stove. A chair stood at a table. Front of them was a

102

battered brass bed with a lumpy blanket. Amy grimaced. Fugate wanted a lungful of fresh air.

Gurley leered at them, warily, maliciously. He was repulsive. They looked at each other. He was loathsome. And hostile. She said, "Let's get out of here."

"You're a proprietor of what, Mr. Gurley?" asked Fugate.

"My cabin," said Gurley. "Naturally."

"Well, that's nice. How big a settlement is it?"

"Me," said Gurley. "Only me. Kilburns Postoffice."

"You're the postmaster?"

"They tell me, but I don't know why. Breaks, caves, buttes. The edge of the country, ten mile deep. Bats and vultures."

"Humans?" asked Fugate.

"A few. They come and go."

"We passed a town a while back," said Fugate. "Met a party that hails the same neck of this woods, a Mr. Foster Kilburn. Kilburn like your post office."

"I recollect him. He come for a letter. Twice, I think."

"What did he look like?"

"I keep mislaying my glasses."

"Liar," said Fugate frigidly.

"Don't call me liar," howled Gurley.

Amy said, "Let's get out of here."

"Who is this Foster Kilburn?" repeated Fugate.

"Hit the grit," said Gurley. "Both of you."

They left the cabin. Later, in the wagon, Fugate said, "Want a cold pone?"

"The cabin," said she drowsily. "I itch. I feel fleas under the floor. Gopher fleas. That cabin."

The dawn was raw and gray. Around them were limestone hummocks, spotty with mesquite and mescal. Fugate said, "We'll eat by four-thirty. There'll be grass by six o'clock. Malloy by suppertime." This edge of Stinson County, called The Caves, was known through all Oklahoma as outlaw country. The mesa-flat knolls, their stony sides honeycombed with fissures and cave mouths, stood about them. The sun arose, huge, watermelon red. It was wilting. Amy said, "Phew!"

About five-thirty, Fugate whispered, "A horseman. Easy!" He drew his gun.

A man rode behind a rocky shard toward their wagon.

Fugate replaced his weapon. He said, "Sheriff McBride, Miss Amy Dennis. Having yourself an early morning canter?"

"Miss Amy Dennis, ma'am, Mr. Fugate, suh," said the sheriff. "Salubrious day. Greetings."

"Catching any culprits?" asked Amy respectfully, bashfully, her eyes on the sheriff's badge.

Fugate laid the reins on his lap. He leaned back to socialize, to shoot a little breeze. Amy liked the sheriff, too.

"This here is my front yard," said Sheriff McBride. "And these rocks and cliffs run west to my property line, to my grassland. This was my daddy's old place, since we moved to Malloy. How did it go down at

Kilburns Postoffice? Meet any robbers on the way? Meet Mr. Gurley? How do you like *this* country?"

"Dreadful," said Amy.

"I ran into a hard case killer last evening out at Eastern Seaboard Cattle," said Fugate casually. "Named Dixie."

"Is that so?" said the sheriff. "Sagebrush Dixies are a dime a dozen nowadays. I know about four of them myself."

Fugate recounted the scene of the dead farmer boy in the dry wash at the store in Caddo County three years ago last October. And Dixie, there.

"I'll make a note of it," said the sheriff. "Seaboard Cattle, heh?"

All in a rush, Amy told the sheriff about Kansas, her trip, how Fugate joined up with her.

Sheriff McBride listened carefully, attentively.

Like a lean mother timber wolf, thought Fugate.

"That's about it," said Amy.

They said good-bye.

The sheriff touched his horse and left them.

The trail ascended, narrowed to a canyon floor with blown sand and arid brush and spiraled steeply through sheer limestone walls. Their wheel hubs jostled and bumped the talus, the piles shaly against the cliffs. About half an hour later, still climbing, they came out on a ledge covered by a bluff. Just ahead of the wagon tongue was the remnants of a campfire, two days old, maybe, with the print of the coffeepot still in it.

They got down. Fugate hunkered over the ashes.

He stood up. He peered intently, here and there, at the ground. A cow pony, four new shoes. A cowboy's worn broken boot soles. Fugate picked up a little round piece of cardboard, about the size of a quarter with a hole in it. "You know what this is?"

He handed it to her. It was a Bull Durham tag.

"I've seen them enough to know," Amy said.

Fugate said, "A Bull Durham tag. A tramp or an outlaw. Outlaw, likely, for the horse is a cow pony. When he had emptied the tobacco bag he raveled the chain stitching, saved the cotton thread and the muslin rag because they are useful in many ways to a man on the trail. He didn't need the tag."

"What was he doing here, do you think, the outlaw?"

"He had his business."

"But why here?"

"I can't keep from thinking about the Seaboard Cattle Ranch. Big ranches like Seaboard are good hideouts. Hands come and go. Not too many questions of a man. I've seen outfits like this before."

They watched a whiptail lizard sunning on a boulder.

"With these outlaws, Mr. Gurley is in danger," said Amy. "It is sure not safe in hills and rocks and stuff."

They mounted the seat. The wagon bed slewed, slid upward, the axles groaned.

A little later, they reached the summit, a plateau with chaparral. They crossed the little plateau, moved over the further rim, a stony saddle ridge, and descended a gradual drop. Afterward they went slowly down a long slope, entered a barranca, a deep gulley, and came through cottonwoods. Suddenly there was the grass.

"I like grass," said Amy. "But I don't like rocks."

Fugate grinned.

Before long they passed a mesa to the northwest. "Eastern Seaboard," said Fugate. "Remember. That's it. The buildings are behind the mesa. Here north and west, it is Company land." A small covey of white-winged doves pelted through the spokes, hovered and settled down a dozen yards away. After a bit they came to two low weedy hills, a marshy swale between them rank with vegetation and stagnated spring water.

They pulled into a saucerlike hollow. At the edges of the banks were wind-gnarled junipers, willows and poplar saplings. There was a reedy pond in the middle, with turf all around growing up to the trees. Everywhere there was sumac. Two horses, a bay and the yellow horse with the roached white mane that Fugate had seen at dusk yesterday at the trough, were tied to a bough of a tree in the shade. Not far away were Mr. Brace and Dixie. The men came forward and Fugate and Amy stopped.

"Good morning," Amy said. Fugate was silent.

"Do you see any water hemlock around here, madam?" the citified man asked. The boss all right, mused Fugate. Look at that dandified mane.

"I don't know what it looks like," she said.

"Bushy weeds. Five or six feet tall. Purplish stems," Fugate said. The Seaboard men ignored him.

Mr. Brace said, "It kills calves. They eat it. It should be grubbed out."

"They call it back home Spotted Cowbane," Amy said. "I don't see any here."

"I don't either," said Fugate.

Dixie picked up an herb and tossed it away. "That ain't one." It was soapwort. Not anything like water hemlock.

"I was riding by a few minutes ago," said Mr. Brace. "I saw the bay back here in the hollow. Dixie was standing around in weeds."

"I saw one," Dixie said, dubiously.

Mr. Brace bowed. "I'm Brace, the manager of this spread, and Dixie here is one of my hands. It sure is a fine day." He beamed.

"Live somewheres around here?" Dixie asked.

Mr. Brace spoke up. "I've seen you somewhere. Where?"

"We saw him last night at the office," Dixie said.

"I remember. He was asking for directions," Mr. Brace said. "Directions for Kilburns Postoffice. I recall, I think. I'm a busy man."

"Right," Dixie said. "Busy, Mr. Brace."

A horseman came down the left bank through the willows, dismounted and joined them. His broken soles made imprints in the miry earth. His roan wore a set of new shoes. He looked furtive and cunning. His eyes were shrunken, his cheeks prison pale. He was bare armed and wore a mangy wolfskin jerkin. His green corduroy pants were drooping and oversized. At his side was a new Navy Colt. He said, "Lady and gentlemen, good morning."

Amy said, "Good morning."

Fugate, Dixie and Mr. Brace nodded. Warily.

The intruder said, diffidently, "I saw the willow tops above the hill here. Willows mean water. Water is what me and my horse need."

"This is brackish water," Mr. Brace said.

Dixie asked, "Do I know you?"

"They call me Shorty. I'm looking for work. I've heard Eastern Seaboard uses a lot of men."

He spoke to Fugate. "I saw you once in South Dakota, didn't I?"

"That depends," said Fugate, affably.

"This water is brackish," Mr. Brace repeated. "The buildings are not far from here. Visitors are always welcomed. Help yourself to water and a little hot victuals. But there are no jobs right now."

Dixie said, "We need several hands right now, Mr. Brace, sir."

"You think we do?" Mr. Brace said.

"If you say so, boss, sir," Dixie replied.

"I believe we do," Mr. Brace said.

"Well, I sure trust your judgment," Dixie said. "I'll take the new hand, Shorty, back with me right now."

"That's a fine yellow horse," said Shorty.

"Yes," said Mr. Bruce, flattered.

Dixie and the stranger rode off together.

Fugate and Amy started off. As they left the hollow, Mr. Brace was still looking around for hemlock.

Last night at the ranch watering trough, Fugate thought, Dixie didn't want any floaters. Now he is hiring one.

This is Dixie's replacement for his gunman, Lawson, Fugate thought.

Dixie had been waiting to meet Shorty here.

Then Brace came along, and then we stumbled in.

The campfire on the ledge this morning. The freshly shod horse tracks. The broken sole boot prints. And now.

This hollow. Eastern Seaboard ranch.

It's just going round and round, decided Fugate, Kilburns Postoffice, Mr. Gurley, the postmaster, outlaws, Dixie, the hermit.

Amy said "Nice people, aren't they?"

Fugate looked straight ahead, his face blank.

CHAPTER
ELEVEN

The sun's heat lay on them in suffocating layers. What would it be like at noon, Fugate wondered?

They passed groups of feeding Seaboard cattle and came to a barbed wire gate, with wire on either side stretching into the distance. Fugate undid the latch. Amy drove through, Fugate fastened the gate. Fugate hopped up.

A half an hour went by. As they went along, the cattle all seemed to have various brands. This was different from Seaboard, Amy thought. "The owner of this land, whoever he is, rents pasturage," Fugate said. "It's mighty good grass. He should wear it out."

They drove over a soddy hump, down a declivity covered with bluestem, and to a cottage yard. The chimney was askew. The windows were empty, uncurtained. The picket fence was half fallen.

A man sat on a slat-bottomed chair in the shade in a little porch, resting by a snowberry bush. It was Sheriff McBride.

"Well, hello!" Sheriff McBride called. "Get down and sit. This is our old family place that I told you about." He gestured with despairing affection at its collapsed condition. "She ain't in very good shape."

Amy and Fugate got down from the wagon. Fugate tied the team to a fence post.

They sat on the porch step.

Sheriff McBride said, "We have been grazing out the land. We have sort of let the place go."

A sweet water creek lay behind the barn, pebbly and shallow, in a plot of alders, caroling with birds. Grass seed burned under the soft wind, malty and honeyed. Amy could see and feel the ground wind come, be still, then move again. Huge white clouds stood stationary against the dense blue sky. She felt enchanted, surrounded with the loveliness of it all.

Sheriff McBride stared sadly at the broken down corral. "Sorry lookin'," he murmured.

"It could be fixed," announced Fugate.

"When I was a boy I had some good times in that corral."

"Yes, I know," Fugate said.

Amy spoke. Fugate and the sheriff waited indulgently.

She said, "That is a fine, A-1 smokehouse, there."

"Yes, ma'am," said the sheriff, pleased. "Cedar. Carted twenty-five miles away. My pa built it."

Amy was lost in thought. "It needs a pigpen on the northwest corner. How did they ever forget that. A pigpen."

The sheriff seemed surprised.

Amy went on. "And, at the northeast corner of the barn, ten beehives."

Fugate gazed on the nonexistent hives.

The sheriff paused. "My brother Floyd and me," he said. "We own it together. Share and share alike. You met Floyd at the courthouse in the county clerk's office. He is the county clerk."

"Yes. I am acquainted with Mr. McBride, and I am acquainted with his setter," said Fugate.

"His setter's name is Twelve Gauge," the sheriff said. "He is worth two dogs or more anytime."

"Amy certainly seems taken with the place," Fugate said. "How much would you ask for it?"

"About ten thousand, and that is reasonable," Sheriff McBride answered. "The land and the buildings go together. I would make easy terms for her, too. Maybe she could pull out of all that trouble she told me about. And I think my ma would like it this way."

Fugate looked solemn.

The sheriff said, "She will have to buy cattle and fix up the buildings. I will talk to the bank about that."

Fugate and Sheriff McBride shook hands.

Amy interrupted them coldly.

"I thank you, Sheriff McBride," she said. "But the Dennises pay their way. I can't pay mine. This place is what I want but I can't do it this way. Thank you kindly."

They gaped at her, aghast.

The three of them talked for a little while, talked about things in general, the tree in front of the house, the sheriff's horse, Fugate's horse, Amy's team, the heat and the time of day. "We better get back to Malloy," said Amy at last.

The sheriff said, "Go two blocks south of the courthouse and you will come to Market Alley. There is an old brick building with an attached stable on the northeast corner. It isn't used much for anything. Because of your emergency, you have my permission to use the whole building."

Fugate said, "You are a kind man, Sheriff McBride."

"There is a good well for your own use and the horses'," the sheriff continued. "Nobody will trouble you; you will have to supply your own food and feed for your horses."

"I don't know whether you are doing too much for us or not," said Fugate. "But we are going to have to take it."

Amy said, "You are certainly a good friend to us, Sheriff McBride. We certainly thank you."

"I will see you in town tonight," Sheriff McBride said. "Adios."

Amy and Fugate ate their dinner. Fugate sat possessed with the thought of their being pursued.

As late afternoon came on, they were in the outskirts of Malloy.

As they passed the courthouse they saw Mr. Gurley, the postmaster, standing by the hitching rail. Fugate reined up beside him, stopped. Amy looked away in revulsion. "Did you say something?" called Fugate.

"Not me," said Mr. Gurley.

He stared at them in recognition. An aromatic haze of town whiskey hung over him.

Mr. Gurley was shaggy haired, uncouth, a bear come out of hibernation. He wore tea-colored, cheap tweed pants and a dirty gray laborer shirt. His vehicle was a hickory platform with buggy wheels. There was a rocking chair bolted down in the middle of the plaform.

114

In the chair there was an old bed pillow. A stumpy mare with shredded harness was hitched to the contraption.

"How goes it back at Kilburns Postoffice?" Fugate asked.

Mr. Gurely said, "You two. Here."

Fugate waited.

"Running. Here and there," said Mr. Gurley. "Like jackrabbits."

"Have you just come?" said Fugate. "Or are you leaving?"

Mr. Gurley ignored him. He turned to Amy. "Your team seems mighty fresh and nice."

"We never press them," Amy answered. She didn't want to talk.

"Do you ever get letters at your post office for a man named Spanton?" Fugate asked.

"No."

"We passed him this morning," Fugate said, "going to Eastern Seaboard."

"Is that so? I don't know him."

"Do you know a man named Dixie?" said Fugate.

"Everybody knows a Dixie in Malloy," said Mr. Gurley. "But me."

He stooped and fiddled with a hamstrap.

"Giddap," said Fugate, clucking to his horses.

"That's that," Amy said.

Later, they called to a bystander and came to a corner. A brick building on Market Alley hove into sight, its panes broken, its sills marred and splintered. In a window was a large piece of red cardboard with black letters: *No Trespassing*.

Fugate jumped down, opened the doors. Amy drove in. He shut a latch behind them.

Fugate patted the wagon fondly. "You are a wonder. You've been through creeks and woods. And look at you."

Amy hopped down beside him.

It was almost dark. The heavy stalls at the far end showed it to be a stable. Before the stalls were two gravel dump carts and a road grader.

He rummaged in their wagon. He lit candles. He said to Amy, "Here is a light for you. I'll be right back." He left.

Fugate reconnoitered. He went from room to room. He looked in and around everything. A dusty office, empty except for a stove and a calendar on the wall. A storeroom, tools piled in one corner. Broken boxes stacked up on a staircase in the stable.

Amy was glad to see him.

He described the layout to her; she listened attentively.

They got to work. Fugate unharnessed the horses. The last stall was about three feet from the back wall. There was a door there. Fugate opened the door and took the horses outside. Great black clouds rolled across the moon. He emptied the stagnant water from the trough and filled it with fresh water from the rusty pump. He watered the horses. Inside, he turned them into their stalls.

116

Fugate got grain out of the wagon. He put it in the manger of each horse. Amy, in the meanwhile, lit the lamp, swept and dusted and put blankets in the office for her and in the storeroom for Fugate. She had taken coal from the bin and had a fire going in the stove. Supper was cooking: cracking bread and coffee. When Fugate stepped in the light and warmth, it seemed very good.

"I'm hungry," he said.

"It is about ready."

Fugate brought in boxes. He and Amy sat down.

After a bit, she said, "I can't feed you a piece of elderberry, doggone it."

Shorty Spanton and Dixie stepped into the room, their guns full cocked.

"Where did they come from?" said Amy.

"They must have come by the watering trough, through the stable," said Fugate.

Fugate and Amy acted as if their visitors were not there.

She asked, "What do they want?"

"We know too much," he said.

The encroachers lunged forward. Fugate killed them.

CHAPTER
TWELVE

The crowd came and went, and Amy and Fugate were again alone. Sheriff McBride and his brother Floyd were there. The town marshal was there. Mr. Brace was in the throng. Gurley, the postmaster, and loafers from the saloon nearby were there. The undertaker and his three helpers were there. Amy's face was white and drawn, her arms held stiffly to her sides. Fugate stood detached and grim.

Fugate heard Mr. Brace talking to the sheriff.

"This Shorty Spanton was new to your outfit?" said the sheriff. "When did you hire him?"

"This morning."

"Was he a pal of Dixie's?" asked the sheriff.

"They had come into town set for mischief, I guess," said Mr. Brace.

"You mean prowling around and thieving and pilfering," said Sheriff McBride.

"I don't know about that, but I have never had any trouble with Dixie," said Mr. Brace.

The undertaker and his three helpers took the bodies out of the room. One of the loafers said, "Here today and gone tomorrow."

Mr. Gurley said philosophically, "They got what was coming to them."

This was the way they came and went.

Amy and Fugate sat down on their boxes. Amy got up and went out to the wagon. She came back with a big square blue bottle and a jelly glass. She poured half a glass. She said, "Drink this."

"What is it?" he said. He drank it.

"Papa sometimes took this when he had been under a strain. When he fixed the smokepipe, or our jersey had her first calf."

Fugate read the label on the bottle. *Mother Coningby's Cure, Jaundice, Scrofula, Palsy, Puerperal Fever, etc., 87% Alcohol.*

No wonder, he thought, eighty-seven percent.

He said, "Why don't you take some?"

"No thank you," Amy said.

Sheriff McBride called through the door, entered, sat on a box Fugate offered and made himself at home. Fugate sat on the floor in a corner.

"I hope you young people are comfortable," said the sheriff.

"We are," Amy said.

No one mentioned the two dead men.

Fugate said, "Sheriff McBride, I would like to ask you something."

"Let's hear it," said the sheriff. "I think we should powwow."

Fugate stressed again all the things that had been happening to Amy. It had really started in Kansas

119

before she and her father left home. This was what it came to.

"So here is what I want to ask you," said Fugate.

"Five miles west of a village called Sheep Jaw is a sorry old deserted house. Do you know it, or anything about it?" He hesitated. "Amy and I stopped there."

"I know the place well," Sheriff McBride said. "It is in my county. It's called the 'old murder house.' People steer away from it. I don't like that place."

"Where an osage thicket is?"

"That's it."

"Two men turkey snared us there," said Amy. "We escaped."

"Who were they?" asked the sheriff.

"It was night," said Amy. "We hid."

"One was Dixie, surely," Fugate said. "I couldn't make out the other. They aimed to butcher us."

"The miscreants, the verminous miscreants," growled the sheriff.

He got up and departed.

Amy said, "I think it's time we get ready for the night."

"Let's do it this way," Fugate said. "I'll sleep in the wagon seat where I can look after our things. I'll keep a careful watch on the horses. Too many people have been coming and going. You sleep in here with your blanket. Keep your rifle by your side."

"That's a wonderful plan," Amy said.

"We will not have to keep this up," Fugate said.

He seemed fatigued.

She asked, "What became of papa's money?"

"Dixie could have taken it."

"Where is it now?"

"I bet it's hidden in the old murder house," Fugate said.

Amy said, "Do you think so?"

"They tried to kill us to keep us from finding out," Fugate said. "Twice they tried to kill us."

"You had better quiet down and get some rest," Amy said.

"You will be safe here. I am going to saddle up and go out to that house now," Fugate said.

"No," Amy said. "Please wait until morning."

Postmaster Gurley lurched drunkenly into the room, a plaid horse blanket over his shoulder. He dropped his blanket at his feet. "My bed," he said. "Howdy, all."

"What in the hell!" Fugate said.

"My gracious me alive!" said Amy.

Fugate got up and stood in front of Gurley.

Gurley said, "I put my mare at the livery barn. I'm on the town. I'm hooked in a stud game. At the saloon. It may last all night."

"Mr. Gurley, you should go back to Kilburns Postoffice," said Amy. "Where you belong is home."

"Why did you come *here?*" Fugate asked.

"The rumor is going around," Gurley said, "that the two of you are living here for a while. I thought I could spend the night."

Mr. Gurley picked up Fugate's coffee cup and poured himself coffee from the pot on the stove. There was a piece of skillet bread left over. He took that.

When he had finished, he departed.

"Bring your things, Amy," Fugate said. "You can sleep on the wagon seat, and I'll sleep in the back."

He was in a state of barely controlled wrath.

They took the lamp with them. "Good night," they said, together. Amy climbed on the wagon bench. Fugate blew out the light.

He went to the front door and tested the latch. He remembered having locked the back door before Dixie and Shorty appeared, but then he'd had to unlock the back door when he went for the sheriff. Now he must lock it again even if he had to let the postmaster in later. How had Dixie and Shorty gotten in?

He went to the stairs and up to the top past the boxes. By the light of a match, he looked into an empty space with long fingers of dust reaching down from the rafters. A door was at the far end of the room. The match went out. He moved without making a sound toward the faint piping of light around the jamb.

Fugate reached the door. He felt for the knob. He found the jamb had been splintered, the mortised lock jimmied. He opened the door. On the threshold was a cabinetmaker's fifteen-inch screwdriver. This was how Dixie and Shorty had entered the building.

Outside the door was a landing with banisters. Steps went down the side of the brick wall. Clouds still swept across the harsh bright moon. Below was what must have been the old marketplace.

It was deserted. Fugate went down to the court.

Under the stairs stood two horses.

"Hello there, old fellows," he said.

He knew them both; Amy and he had seen them in the hollow at Eastern Seaboard.

The bay had been there when they came. Shorty got there later on the roan.

Now Fugate checked the roan's new shoes. On Dixie's bay was a pair of pommel bags. He threw them across his shoulder.

He went up the steps, through the attic and down into the stable.

Fugate went to the front of the wagon. By the light of a candle he saw Amy was safe; she was sound asleep.

Some distance away, he sat down on the earth. By the unsteady wick, he unbuckled the first pommel bag. A can of Copenhagen snuff. An Indian feathered talisman. A package of playing cards. A broken poker chip. A phial of gun oil. A harmonica with some sprung metallic reeds. A pants' button. Fourteen licorice drops.

Fugate opened the second pommel bag. An old shirt bundled up. In the shirt, he found a sock with a letter in it. It was addressed: *Mr. Henry Dawes, Kilburns Postoffice, Oklahoma. c/o Postmaster.* Dixie.

The letter said:

> H.H. Flood & Son
> Dealers in Real Estate
> 119 Dauphine Street
> New Orleans
> Louisiana

Dear Mr. Dawes:

In response to your inquiry concerning a saloon, there is a good one in New Orleans listed with me. A sizable structure in excellent repair. One front room with bar, in the back three rooms. Upstairs, a room and cubbyhole. The furniture and equipment go with the property. The place is still rather well stocked. The owner is retiring.

Let me hear from you. I shall be glad to be of service to you in this matter.

Obligingly,
H. H. Flood

Fugate stashed the pommel bag in the wagon. He snuffed the candlewick and waited.

In the dawn light from the stable windows objects began to appear, the stalls, the wagon.

The back door was being rattled noisily. Fugate went to let the postmaster in.

"I won sixteen dollars!" Mr. Gurley shouted.

Fugate guided him into the office and showed him his horse blanket.

"You denied knowing Dixie," Fugate said.

"That's right. Postmasters don't talk."

"But Dixie's dead now," Fugate said.

"I didn't know him anyhow. He just mailed several letters and got a few."

With his boots still on, Mr. Gurley wrapped himself in his blanket and began to snore. Fugate left the room. Roosters crowed all over the town. Every house had its chicken yard. In the plains and hills there was no such sound.

Fugate woke Amy. She went out to the pump. When she came back in, her face was moist and shining, her hair rearranged. He watered the horses and then fed them.

"Let's get ready to travel," he said. "Sheep Jaw, the osage thicket, the murder. We're driving fast."

"Fast?"

"We'll eat as we drive."

"What about Mr. Gurley?" Amy said.

"There is food and coffee in there."

Someone was walking in the attic.

Sheriff McBride came down the steps into the stable.

He said, "Hail, Miss Amy! Have a good slumber, ma'am? You look as pretty as a red shoe. You been up all night, Mr. Fugate? You look all wore out. I just met a couple a saddle mounts in the old marketplace out there."

CHAPTER
THIRTEEN

"What are you doing here, Sheriff?" exclaimed Amy.

"Just promenading around," Sheriff McBride said. "Dixie's and Shorty's horses were not where I thought they would be. The Eastern Seaboard men always stay overnight at the Crystal Eatery. Two rooms are there for any of the ranch outfit to put up in. But their horses were not there, they are here."

Fugate went to the wagon for the pommel bags. "These bags were on Dixie's bay." Fugate got the letter out of the sock and showed it to Sheriff McBride. The sheriff studied the letter.

Fugate said, "Did Dixie have money?"

"They say he was poor as dirt," the sheriff replied. "No cowhand ever has money."

"Why was he interested in buying a saloon in New Orleans?" asked Fugate.

"Search me!" said Sheriff McBride.

"He was going to use *my* money!" Amy said. "He has hidden it at the old house!"

"Let's get going!" Fugate said sharply.

They had been talking softly, almost in whispers. Postmaster Gurley joined the group; he was a hermit, he lived in seclusion. "You woke me up!" he said. "I never heard such a hullabaloo. Laughin' and bellerin' and cutting up like hyenas."

They gazed fixedly at him. The sheriff looked astounded.

Fugate said, "Mr. Gurley, you know what I think? I think Dixie and you were close friends."

"I don't recall," said Mr. Gurley. "Sometimes cow-pokes drop in and play a game of checkers with me."

"Tommy rot," said Fugate.

"I'm absentminded," said Mr. Gurley.

Fugate said, "He's lying in his teeth."

"You're talking to the *law* now, Mr. Gurley," said the sheriff gruffly. "Don't perjure at me."

"Dixie sent and received mail for about a year and a half at my post office," said Mr. Gurley.

"What kind of mail?" Fugate asked.

"He wrote to a few magazines," said Mr. Gurley. "He got personal letters from all around the country. Two or three dozen in the year and a half. There was one left on the wall desk in the post office. Evidently he had opened and read it and forgot it. The letter was from a man in Ohio. He enclosed a classified ad from a farm paper and wanted to know more about the advertised ranch." Mr. Gurley seemed puzzled. "What were they talking about? But Dixie must have put ads like that in all those magazines."

"Bait for emigrants," Fugate said. "Religious and farm magazines."

"We took one," said Amy. "*The Kansas Swine Breeder.*"

"Your father could have read the ad," Fugate said. "That was the lure that brought him out here."

"I'll take it up from here," said McBride.

Fugate harnessed the team. Amy, who had already gotten in, picked up the reins. Fugate slid open the heavy front door.

Mr. Brace edged in through the stable door.

His hands were scrubbed, his ears powdered, his collar and cuffs clean, his boots well blackened. So early in the day. How long had he been up? It took time to be dressed like that.

He looked alarmed and recoiled when he saw the sheriff and Mr. Gurley.

"Quite a gathering for this time of day," Mr. Brace said. "How are you, sheriff? And Postmaster Gurley?"

"I think I'll finish my sleep," Gurley remarked. He looked sultry, glum.

"I found your horses," said Sheriff McBride.

"What can I do for you?" said Fugate. "We're fixing to leave."

"I am going back to the ranch in a few minutes," Mr. Brace announced, "and I would like to engage the young lady as my housekeeper. The house is just too much for me. The money will be good and the work easy." He looked at Amy. "How about it?"

"No," Amy said.

Fugate gave Mr. Brace a glassy, motionless glare.

"You know what, Mr. Brace," he said. "I think you were there that night at the old house by the osages. You took our wagon and team." He spoke inertly. "You and Dixie."

128

"What in the world are you talking about?" Brace said.

"Do you know a man by the name of Lawson?" said Fugate.

"Not that I remember."

"He worked for you sometime back at Eastern Seaboard, didn't he?"

"There have been a procession of hands at Eastern Seaboard," said Brace.

"I knew Lawson," said Sheriff McBride. "By sight. He went around with two other Seaboard hands. One of the men was a wicked looking hombre and rode a reddish brown horse. His other pal wore a striped coat. Lawson was the third man. He wore tight, smooth leather chaps and a gray shirt. The three always rode together."

"You are mistaken. I don't think they were my men," said Mr. Brace.

"They will be on your payroll ledger," said Fugate. "They may be listed under extra sums of money payed out. Accounts at stores in town for sure."

"They were the three men that killed my papa," Amy said. "I saw them. And Mr. Fugate saw them. Mr. Fugate helped bury Papa."

Mr. Brace was desperate.

Fugate said, "The clerk at the *Padgett House* can identify you." Sheriff McBride moved over to where Brace stood.

"You were behind of all this," said Fugate. "Not just what happened to Amy and me. Robberies and killings.

You directed them all. Everything that took place led back to you. It was all done under your orders."

"Why?" the sheriff said.

"Because he is a gross criminal," Fugate said. "He must steal from his company, too."

"We will see about *that*," said Sheriff McBride.

Mr. Brace's face went ashen and twisted.

"Did you swallow your tongue?" asked Fugate.

Sheriff McBride and Mr. Brace walked up the street. Half-asleep, the postmaster left the stable and went back into the office. Amy lifted the reins.

"Wait a minute," called Fugate.

He went to the rear of the wagon. He climbed over the tailboard. Most wagons have the toolbox outside. Mr. Dennis's toolbox was inside, ironed with strips to the side of the wagon bed.

Why was Mr. Brace still interested in Amy?

The money had to be here. He raised the lid of the box. The gear was all there: a coil of rope, an ax, a little cloth with extra kingbolts and linchpins, an auger, nails. And a tin drum of axle grease.

More important than food to a traveler are his tools and axle grease.

He opened the drum of grease, picked up an auger and moved the auger through the axle grease. He struck something on the bottom of the drum.

Then, suddenly, he had a golden coin in his hand.

"We got it!" yelled Fugate.

"What?" called Amy.

"The gold," cried Fugate. "Your papa's money. We had it all along."

About a month later they sat on Amy's porch, the sheriff, Fugate and Amy.

With the money, Amy had bought the sheriff's mother's farm. The deed had been registered. Fugate and Amy had been busy. The pillars on the porch were straight. The snowberry bush had been trimmed and mulched. The fence had no missing pickets and stood upright. The panes of white curtained windows were spotless. The chimney had been repaired.

At the barn, pigs were happy in their new pen. Amy's herd was on the way.

Sheriff McBride was proud. "You certainly had a nice little wedding. You done fine."

"At Eastern Seaboard, Brace and Dixie did not recognize Amy and did not connect me," said Fugate, "with the situation. Later they put two and two together."

The sheriff looked grave.

"In the end Dixie almost had enough money to have bought the New Orleans saloon. With Amy's money, he would have clinched the deal."

They shook their heads.

"Brace got the surprise of his life early that morning on seeing you, Sheriff McBride, at the stable. He had come to kill Amy and me and get the money. You being there blocked it. On the spur of the moment, he trumped up the story about Amy being his housekeeper."

The sheriff said, "How did Brace get the money from people? Did they send it to him or did they bring it?"

"It could have been both ways," Fugate said. "As soon as Brace heard Amy's father had his money ready, he sent his gunmen. Maybe that was the way."

"What was Dixie's part in it all?" said the sheriff.

"He was Brace's man. He found other gunmen and helped plan things," said Fugate.

"Dinner is ready," said Amy. "Let's go in. Roast pork."

"Pig," said Fugate patiently to the sheriff.